Cansir

Tkay TheAuthor

ISBN-10:153518955X
ISBN-13:9781535189552

DEDICATION

Thank you everyone! It has been a tremendous journey transitioning and establishing myself. Without the hard-work and inspiration of family this project would be incomplete. I thank you and appreciate your love & support. Please continue to follow me as this is only the beginning

"No weapon formed against me shall prosper"

Tkay TheAuthor & Productions EST. 2016

Published Author of: Tears of Purpose

Cansir
&
Bravery is Beauty (Soon II be released)

Biography

Tkay TheAuthor is an urban fiction novelist. In her day-time she works for the county of Erie as a "Adult Protective Case Worker" specializing in assisting people from all walks of life. Her knowledge and ability to implement both the "Social Workers Code of Ethics" & "PEER Ethics" assist her with doing above quality work.. Tkay TheAuthor is a hard working mom and loves serving the community. She is very implementive in seeing other women and youth become entrepreneurs, while managing family, work, and her own purpose related ambitions. She not only an instrument, but a vessel to the communities in which she serves. You can visit her at www.tkaytheauthor.com for contact information, debuts, and promotions! She is guaranteed to deliver quality and professional services while projecting the image of a true role model.

CONTENTS

ACKNOWLEDGMENTS

Thank you everyone! It has been a tremendous journey transitioning and establishing myself. Without the hard-work and inspiration of family this project would be incomplete. I thank you and appreciate your love & support. Please continue to follow me as this is only the beginning

The Introduction:

How this all started I really don't know.

How this all ends, only God can say so!

All I can ask is "Can I live"?

Not sure of what I may have done to deserve this shit!

XOXOXO,

LONDON

10/10/09

8

Noooo, Slap!

Noooo, Slap!

Please Dorian stop!

Bitch didn't I fucking tell you not to talk to that nigga. I don't give a fuck who he is!

But he's your brother!

And you fucking him, ain't you! Don't lie bitch cause, I know! All the signs are there! You aint shit! (Dorian kicks London in her face and spits on her before walking away).

Whyyyyyy! Whyyyyy! Heeeelp me.....somebody please help me (LONDON BEGINS TO PRAY).

Mommy! (HER DAUGHTER SCREAMS).

No,no,no baby it's okay! Mommy's going to be just fine! Now shhh! Please, okay!

Mommy no please, let me call the police. Please mommy! I don't want to lose you mommy! Noooooooooo! London's daughter cries loudly enough for her brother to hear.

Ma!He calls out in an abrupt but stern voice

Ma! Please let me her son yells with intent to threaten.

I'm going to kill this.

Silence quickly filled the room

*****And now let the story begin! *****

Chapter One

1/2/2009

10:45 PM

Ring...Ring...Ring.

Hello!

Hey! Girl what's up?

Shit, bored!

Yeah me to honestly.

Crazy how it's really nothing to do, but sit here on "Facebook"!

True!

Hey why don't we all go out and have a drink?

Who is this we, we speak of?

Me, you and Nye. She just hit me up on the book, bored doing pretty much of nothing her damn self, so I suggested we hang out!

Well alrighty then. Wait who's driving?

Sky, I will! Get ready!

Shower steaming. Pandora popping! "Nikki Manaj" song "Your Love" blasting.

Okay, okay, okay! Pussy clean! Breath smelling good, and this Italian body in my hair is on point. Damn! It's been a long time since I've been out, and shit I'm jive looking good. That pussy ass nigga Dorian can eat a dick! I hope the bitch he with fuck I'm in his ass with a dirty dildo! hahahaha! I'm cute! (puckers lips and blows a kiss to self).

Ring! Ring! Ring!

Hello!

Hey Sissy!

What's up Nye?

Can you do me a huge favor pleeeeeeeeeease!

What?

Bring me a pair of leggings when you pick me up.

What color?

Any will be fine. I'm throwing an all-black sweater dress on, and BABY! Nye says sounding excited adding a higher pitch to her voice.

Kool! I'm almost ready so tell Sky be looking out, Ill grab her first.

Okay bye! Love you sissy!

Ayeeeee! Okay ladies where are we on our way to tonight?

Anywhere but nowhere!

Nye shut your ass up! Stop one the Nugget! We can go in there to get a drink or two first, while more than likely we won't even be paying for shit! We're young, cute, and those old men cater to new faces daily.

Right! Hell you know them old ass, lonely fucking grand pa's in there are sure to get us popped.

Bet!

"Set it off on the left yal, set it off on the right yal, set it off, set it off, set it off, set it off, set it off, set it off"

Bartender! (Sky shouts out). Can I get a triple shot of gin with a side of cranberry, 2 lemons, a lime, and sweet and sour mix?

Damn baby. You sure can. Shit after that drink where you going?

Not with your old ass! Now mix it up right grand pa and I might tip you. Hahahahaha! London and Nye what you drinking?

Give me goose and cranberry, London replies.

I'll take chardonnay, Nye says.

Okay ladies that'll be $27.00

First round on me says a tall slim fella with a navy blue "Pelle Pelle" jacket on, standing up smacking a crispy $50dollar bill on the bar.

Thank you, all three of the ladies chimed in, in unison!

No ladies thank you! My pleasure!

After round two Sky says we out! I'm ready to meet me a killer.

A killer? Nye & London both look at Sky confused saying a killer?

Yup a nigga that can kill this pussy! Hahahahaha!

Yoooo! Who's that right there?

I don't know but we can damn sure find out. Shit it's slippery as hell out here and all this black ice is a mother, but I bet I bust this U-turn.

Bet! Bust-it baby!

Nye shut up!

Whatever!

Watch out! Damn!

What happened?

Didn't you just see that nigga trying to run across the street and busted his ass, right in front of your truck. Look down!

Fool, that's what he get! Girl he got friends though. You see them trying to help his drunk ass up. I want whatever he had.

Sky believe me you don't need any of what he had. Hahahahaha. Let's go! Oh and Sky whatever you do, please don't drink any shit blue!

Fuck you bitch!

Uh no, I believe that's what happened after you drank that blue shit the last time. Who accompanied your ass drinking blue-shit, then happily made their way home with you? Tywan was it? Oh okay, don't get me started.

Hey shorty what's good, a big 250 pound plus well- groomed fine ass man approaches London smelling like "Fahrenheit" said. You going in here?

Yes! London was surprised.

Good you coming in with me then!

Sorry folks were closing shortly, and unfortunately we're at capacity, the gentleman working the door of the bar responded.

Damn!

Damn what?

We out here and cutie, I'm riding with you.

I don't even know your name.

It's Nasir, but you can just call me Sir!

(Suddenly London gets serenaded by Nasir)

"Which one of yal going home with Nasirrrrrrrr"

Really! You think you "Trey Songz" huh?

"I want yo body like right now! You know I live a magnum

Lifestyle".

London suddenly feels a warmth in-between her legs while this teddy bear ass nigga is singing this song. All while London is driving she is thinking to herself. What am I getting myself in to. Suddenly realizing how it had been almost10 months since she felt a man. Now he wasn't her normal type, but as of right now, he was looking right. Fresh cut, nice sneakers, smelling right, and her worse attraction he was. Tear drops tatted on his face with over fifteen tattoos on his body at the time, fresh out of jail not even home 90 days, and looking like he could bust that pussy wide open. Now trying to live life for better and on a positive but damn was a girl feeling like R. Kelly's song "My body's calling". Damn!

London? London? L-o-n-d-o-n!

What was her response with sarcasm invoked!

Girl dang. I see this nigga got you open singing Trizzy Tre and shit huh?

No!

Oh I don't Nasir responded blushing.

I said no didn't I?

Yeah okay, but this song right here! This is my shit! Nasir began placing his big muscular hand on London's thigh while singing: "Can you stand the rain" "Storms will come"!

Oh my God! Stop! Please!

Why? "Storms will come" "This we know for sure" he continues.

Really please. Like not only is this my favorite song, but my all-time favorite group. You rubbing on my leg like this could really get me in trouble and to be polite and honest I rather it not.

So you like "New Edition" huh?

Please! She'd move the Grand Canyon out of the way if she had to, to get to them says Sky.

They are my favorite group to. I see we have a lot in common. I like more and more. Yo! I'm jive hungry. Let's go to Jims

What "Jims Steak-out"?

No, "Jims Truck stop"!

That's cool. Why not? Hell it's late and not much of anything is still open any ways. I see your friend in the car with my man all happy and shit! She definitely must like him. Nye never just ditches me, and especially for a nigga. Hahahaha!

Oh! Well Shorty fuck all that. What's good with you?

Hmph! London didn't totally understand exactly what Nasir was trying to say to her, and her facial expression gave it away.

So what you got a man he just blurted out and asked.

Nah, I just been doing me.

So what you mean by that, you out here?

No I just been trying to get over what I got myself into and pray not to make the same mistakes again.

Hello people! May I take your orders?

Yeah a double order of wings, hot and crispy with an extra blue cheese. A double cheeseburger with seasoned fries, no pickle London and Sky ordered without hesitation..

You sir?

Nothing I'm good.

Okay and you sir?

I'm straight.

Wait! You two aren't going to get anything to eat?

Nah we good.

Okay well I'll put your order in right away! In the meantime what would you like to drink?

Water! They all said in harmony!

Excuse me, London stands up to walk by. I have to go to the bathroom. You good Sky?

Yeah girl I'm fine. He sitting here acting like he mad at the world.

I'm not acting like nothing (Toni, Nasir's friend replied). You just think a nigga supposed to kiss your ass. I don't know shit about you except that you pissy drunk and got a smart ass mouth. Women like you are highly unattractive, and for the most part only good for one thing. Please don't debate me!

Well I never!

Well you never should have drank whatever you did, cause it's got you feeling like wonder woman or some shit. The Pink power ranger or something.

Yo two are a mess. Let me go to the bathroom, in the meantime chill out Toni! We have to be gentlemen tonight!

You mean this morning!

See what I'm talking about Sir. You got the cool one and look what the fuck I get!

What took you so long to get here Nye?

Bitch what was you doing? Your bra strap broke and your leggings on backwards (London smacks Nye on her ass where the tag is).

Girl all I'm going to say is that his dick was rather small but he made up for it. Tell your friend don't drink after him. Hahahahaha!

Oh my God! Un-fucking believable. You are fucking crazy! Girl I have to pee! Yessssssss (London says while relieving herself)! Whew! Lord what have I gotten myself into? We all been drinking. Don't know these dudes from Adam, but the mystery of it is all kind of fun. I know once I get home, I'm going straight to sleep! (London washes her hands and leaves the ladies room).

Yo!

Shit! What you stalking me?

Nah baby girl I was just coming to tell you my mans is ready to go. Yo girl Sky mouth to smart. She done pissed my man off.

How?

While talking shit she threw up all on the table! I believe she out cold right now. I had to walk away. Those two, boy oh boy.

Damn!

Yeah. I took the liberty of having them put your stuff in a to-go box.

Oh okay! Well thank you.

Sure no problem. You wanna exchange numbers?

Sure. 716-253-9887.

Okay and here this is my brother phone. You can call me on this one until I get a phone. 716-334-4276. Call me when you get home so that I know you made it in safe. If I may suggest you might want to take a bag with you for emergency purposes.

I see you got jokes! I will, as I just got my truck detailed anyhow.

Would it be too much to ask you for a hug?

Of course not!

What started out as a hug turned into a kiss! That kiss was

everything. Nasir kissed London so good, she instantly became wet. Nasir knew she was feeling him and all of a sudden he began to feel her to. What started out as fun and games had Nasir thinking. I have to see what that pussy feels like! Fuck it! I'm going home with her!

Nasir whisper's in London's ear: You want me don't you? Listen I want you too. I'm getting in that truck with you and whatever happens, happens when we arrive at our destination okay! London begins to shake. Her body was saying yes with her mind and tongue in unison. London for sure didn't say no, and to the house they went!

I don't want you to get the wrong idea about me, but I don't just go taking men home with me. You my friend are very lucky as it is only due to your sister Jazz that I'm even feeling safe with this.

Do me a favor okay London?

What?

Shut the fuck up and bend that ass over!

Nasir was straight nasty. He took London's ass and spread it open as wide as it would go. Orally pleasing her. He ate her ass from top to the bottom. London's clit began to swell as he nibbled on it sliding 2 fingers in her pussy and 1 in her ass. The double penetration was new for London, but at the same time it felt so good. Nasir eased himself beneath her gabbing her by the waist and gently placed her pussy on his face. He may not have been hungry at Jims but he damn sure ate the-hell out of her pussy.

The shit felt so good London could feel herself transforming. She started popping that pussy in circles and making that ass clap unintentionally by the way she would squeeze her lips on to his tongue and then release. With much base in her voice she begged Nasir to let her up and give her the dick.

Stop! Ohhhhh stop it right now! I need to feel you inside of me now! Daddy please! Oh shit! Where the comments screaming from London's mouth!

Nasir obliged and when he entered in. It was everything he could imagine.

Shit mommy! Damn! What the fuck! Hell yeah. Nasir became a bit frightened as the pussy was so good. It was something unexplainable, and by far everything a man would want and more.

London was so wet that it was easy sailing when inside. London watched how Sir enjoyed her as she enjoyed him. That turned her on even more. That made her feel attractive and secretly wanting him more. She pushed him off top and straddled him in her bitch position. London began to ride him backwards taking his legs and placing his feet on top of her thighs. This gave her extra bounce. As she popped up and down and in a circle, all you could hear was ughhhhhhhhh! Nasir was done he had cum!

Damn! That shit was alright!

Haha! Oh it was just alright huh? I hope they ain't hear us up front?

Damn I forgot they came back with us too! What time is it?

10:17 AM.

Yo I gotta go shortie. I'm a call you though okay, and umm, can I use your bathroom first?

Sure! Towels are in the cabinet behind the door and wash cloths top drawer of the sink. While London lay's in her bed: Ding Dong! Ding Dong! Her door bell begins to ring. As she isn't expecting anyone, she wonders who could it be. Ughh here I come! Damn! London heads to the door in her bathrobe and looks to see who it is. While looking out the peep hole, she looks at both Sky and Toni sprawled out on her couch. What you all didn't hear the doorbell. What yal niggas couldn't answer the door?

Who is it?

It's me sis Jazz!

Toni and Sky begin arguing on the couch. Sis all she wanna do is argue with a young man, like her mouth smart as fuck!

Yeah but you was not saying that shit 30 minutes ago, was you?

Heyyyyyyy, what's good (Jazz speaks when she enters the room)? Toni what the fuck you here too?

Man sis! It's all your brother Nasir fault! Sis London cool, but this woman right here, mouth smart as fuck! She giving me a headache. Shit how you knew to come here anyway?

Shit when I got the call I had to come see what was good!

Hey Pakos Kids! Pakos Kids! Hahahaha! Hey sis (Nasir speaks to Jazz)! I'm ready!

Yeah and this clown ass nigga ready to Jazz! Don't leave him behind at all! This nigga has to go. He not even worthy of being a side piece. While you was in the back getting your back blown out this fool was up here tripping. He asked me to suck his dick and said if I do him he would do me! Like how the fuck old are you, and why would I even think about sucking his raggedy ass dick? This fool got me twisted!

Hahaha! Well what were you up here doing then? I did hear a little noise whenever we would take a quick time-out.

I did only kissed him. Sky takes a long pause and after looking at everyone including Toni's facial expression she said: Okay I let him hit!

Hahaha I knew you two weren't arguing all that time.

Well bitch I don't even have to ask you what you were doing as we heard you all the way out here, and him too!

Hahaha! Welp as the saying goes a lady never tells!

************Later that day************

Ring. Ring. Ring. Hello! Hey beautiful what's up with you?

Uh nothing. Who is this?

Oh you forgot about me that quick huh ma? It's Sir!

Oh okay yes. This isn't the number you gave me, which is why I asked.

Oh yeah, well that's why I'm calling you. I have my own phone now so you can call me on here. What you doing?

Cooking chicken and steak hoagies.

Okay! So you can burn huh? Well put me up one. I'm coming back tonight if it's okay with you. I wouldn't want to step on anyone else's shoes or over step my boundaries.

No that's fine you good.

Cool. Talk to you later!

Hmmmm last night, well this morning was fun. Shit, he actually coming back. I honestly wasn't looking to keep this shit going but what else is there to do. A girl gets bored so I guess some company would be fine.

Ring. Ring. Ring. Hello!

Mom!

Yes.

What you doing?

Working!

What's up?

Ummm can the kids spend the night tonight? I have to go to class earlier than usual (lying).

What time will you be bringing them?

9 pm.

Okay call your dad.

Now London did feel bad, but after what she already experienced the kids damn sure didn't need to hear what was about to go down.

Siyion! You and your sister are going to your grand mas tonight. Start getting your school stuff together. Your food is almost ready okay?

Okay!

Sincere mommy said we going to granny house. I'll come help you pack up your stuff for grannies. Make sure you bring your Nintendo DS, case, pen, and games so you will have something to do! Mommy said we're going to stay the whole weekend to!

Boy stop lying to your sister! You know damn well granny didn't say that! You two think you slick!

Ring. Ring. Ring.

Hello!

What's up girl?

Nothing girl cooking and getting the kids ready to leave.

Leave! Where they going?

My mom's house for the night. Siyion think he slick. He's trying to get his grandmother to let them stay for the week!

Oh okay. That could be nice if they do. Shit, I wish I had that type of opportunity. What you got going on tonight?

Nasir said he was coming back through so I didn't want the kids seeing a new man right now. I Mean shit me and they father been done and he has moved on, but It's different for me, and this is too new to just have my kids around it.

Girl shut up! Ain't shit new about what you doing. You just finally living and getting some dick!

Damn Sky why you have to say it like that?

Cause sometimes you be acting like a granny.

A granny London questions with a slight hesitation before asking. Really?

Yes! Really.

Whatever!

So what time is this nigga coming through? You know it's Sunday and we usually hit the Humboldt Inn.

Right. I'm not sure. I'll text him and see.

Oh you'll text him and see! You really feeling this dude huh?

Yeah maybe Why is it a problem?

No! Not one at all. I can just tell that nigga pipe game right. Hit me up and Let me know what your plans are going to be. I'll be waiting!

*********** Later on that night! ***********

Girl tonight was alright! I'm glad you could make it out! I see you was out there getting it to. Usually you sitting down acting like a granny, but tonight you got on the dance floor and threw that ass in a circle or two. I was so proud watching you in action. It was like old times when we used to go in!

Shut up! I always dance. I can't help if the DJ was on tonight!

Shit you were all the way on tonight. You were breaking it all the way down! Hell that pipe he laid transformed your ass and it shows.

Girl please! Well what you getting into? I see you putting on your lip gloss and shit. It's 3:45 am and you putting on lip gloss. That damn sure doesn't mean you're going to bed.

Damn bitch you observant!

Why wouldn't I be Hell you been observing my ass all night long your damn self. It's only right that I return the favor. SKY! WATCH OUT! What you didn't see that car?

Chill I got this, while still putting on her lip-gloss.

Well whoever you going to creep with must be special while you trying to kill me in the process. Driving and putting on lip gloss.

I'm going over Derricks.

Who is Derrick?

He was the guy smacking on my ass over by the DJ booth. Remember him? You were dancing with his brother.

Oh okay. Yeah he kept trying to give me his number too. Well be safe. Text me when you get there and when you get home. Don't make me come looking for you ready to kill a nigga.

I won't! Alright girl good night.

Ugh lord yes (London sits on the edge of her bed)! Finally! I can take these shoes off. Tonight was fun, but I really could have stayed home. I'm tired as fuck. This shower might be quick, but it will be everything when I'm done. It's 3:30 am and I haven't heard a thing from Nasir. That nigga already fucking up. Well you can't really expect much from a one night stand no how. I guess I should have seen it coming. Thankful for the moment though.

Knock, knock, knock!
Knock, knock, knock!

Who is it? (London steps out of her shower and throws on a towel).

Yooooo! Knock, knock, knock!

Who is it, I said?

Hey boo it's Sin!

Excuse me! I don't do the come by when you feel like it, unplanned, unannounced and swear you getting in shit. Miss me with that sir please and thank you!

I'm sorry. I Really am. I was with my man and had him drop me off. That's why I was knocking so hard. Plus I left my phone in his car and I couldn't call you. He pulled off to quick.

Can I come in?

Damn! I see you was getting ready for daddy huh?

Daddy! No!

Well you was getting ready for something cause, it's 430 in the morning and you all in the shower and shit. Tell that nigga he not getting in tonight!

You funny!

And you pretty! Come here!

Ohhhhhh!

Wait!

No!

Wait!

Okay!

Uhhhhh shit!

Oh my!

What the fuck is going on?

Yeah that ass fits so right on this dick. Ummmmmmm girl this pussy is the shit. Ohhhh! Ummmmm! Sit on my tounge just for a little bit.

Wait it!

Wait what?

Come on and let me nibble on that clique.

Oh damn! We can't keep meeting up like this.

Sluuuuuurp! Why not?

Well uhhhh! Oh! Okay! Ummmm yessssss! Ummmmm.

Now what were you saying? Spread those legs!

Nothing!

What?

Nnnnnothing!

You like this dick don't you?

Yyyessss!

Good cause I like this pussy to!

Damn that was good.

Negative. That was excellent!

Both lay in the bed with different emotions. London begins to wonder if all of what's going on is leading to a relationship, and if so is she ready? Nasir is trying to figure out if London is really the woman he wants to be with. Not really sure of what real love is, but debating if he is ready to find out!

***********Six months later************

So I went to the doctor's today.

Okay and? What you pregnant?

No, but I do now have the nasty fucking pussy disease!

What's that?

What you mean what's that? Shit what's that? I ain't give it to you! I bet I know that!

Yes the fuck you did! Trichomonas's is a STD passed on by niggas like you fucking nasty pussy bitches! Hope you have some Medicaid cause it's obvious that the bitch you fucking don't or just don't get checked out!

Shut the fuck up yo! I'm out! You probably gave me that shit! Remember you fucked me on the first night so who knows.

What? Nigga we been together 6 months and you talking about the first fucking night! Fuck out of here! The way my pussy set up is I'll know in a week. Anything smell different, look different, or even feel different to me and I'm going straight to the clinic!

Man I'm not trying to hear that shit! Like I said you probably gave it to me. It isn't like I didn't know where your pussy was before I started fucking you!

Well then you should have asked if you felt that way, cause you damn sure didn't have a problem sucking the soul out of me either now did you? Yeah cause the cat clearly had your tongue, and while you getting your dick checked out check your mouth!

Look! Do yourself a favor and shut the hell up before you get what you looking for!

Get what I'm looking for, and what's that? Like seriously! It seems I already got something I wasn't looking for so what is it I could be looking for Sir, and I'm not saying your name!

Listen, I'm really not feeling this shit you trying to tell me right now, so I'll just grab my shit and leave. I think I may have made a mistake fucking with you anyhow! You seem a bit childish. Like act more your age instead of your panty size. So you got something wrong with your pussy! As I said previously, how do I know you didn't give that shit to me! Your whole approach was wrong, but no worries. I'll get my dick straight. You worry about your pussy and lose my number while you at it! Duces!

Girl guess the fuck what?

What's up?

This nigga done gave me some shit!

See bitch! I told you he wasn't shit but noooooooo!

Shut up!

Yup so what you going to do now?

Take these meds hoe that's what I'm going do. Shit I'm surprised your ass don't have something. You stay popping that pussy on a nigga.

Bitch you got jokes I see.

Seriously Sky, I'm not laughing.

Awww the poor little baby mad cause her pussy man down!

Really bitch!

I'm just playing girl!

Whatever. Click!

I know this bitch didn't just hang up on me. Well glad she let me know what was up. That nigga isn't shit! She'll call me back later London just mad right now.

Ring, Ring, Ring!

Hello!

Bitch you ain't shit!

Who the fuck is this?

Sir! Fuck you mean who is this?

Oh now you want to call me huh! Why are you mad, cause your girl cussed you the hell out huh?

Bitch you dirty as hell! I'm sure you been aware you had this shit didn't you? I knew some shit was up when I smelled that shit while we were fucking!

Nigga stop acting like a bitch! She crying and now you crying too. Ha, ya both made for each other. That's what the fuck you get for dipping out on my girl.

YOUR GIRL! What is this something yal do?

No! What happened between us should have never fucking happened. Maybe had she kept her mouth shut about how you always dicking her down I never would have been curious.

Yeah well you seemed to be a bit more then curious when you had my dick and my balls in your mouth. I should tell her who I got this shit from. Bet she stop fucking with you before me! Hahahaha, clown ass bitch. I should have my sisters beat your ass!

Click!

*********** Three Days Later ***************

For the life of me I swear I don't know what I've gotten myself into. Now all of a sudden since my pussy foul a nigga MIA! Okay! Bet London get her priorities straight. This exactly what the fuck I get for rushing into yet another relationship.

Ring, Ring, Ring.

Hello!

Hey sissy what's good?

Girl shit, by the way you talked to Sky?

Nope not in like three days. My cousin said that she seen her at Sisters Medical Center.

Isn't Sisters Medical only for treatment with STD's and pregnancy?

I was just joking with Sky three days ago regarding STD's. She okay? She must have received something from the guy she was with as my cousin said he looked pissed.

She was with a guy? Did they say what he looked like?

Just that he was tall, thick and he looked pissed too.

Nah!

Nothing. I was just really thinking out loud.

Well are we still on for crab legs and spades? If so I'll call Jazz and see if Bri wants to replace Sky. I'm going to lay down for a little while and take a quick nap. Call me when your all on your way!

Now I've been knowing Sky for some time and something just isn't sitting right (London talking aloud to herself). I haven't spoken to her in three days, nor him. I just told him about my current situation and hinted to Sky about her pussy. Now either she randomly went out to get checked out or she knew what was already up with her pussy. At least I would like to think that's the case. My intuition says different, but I could be wrong. Hell I'm going to pray I'm wrong, because if my gut proves to be right, that bitch is going to get her ass beat! And that clown ass nigga too! Huh!

************4 AM**************

Tap, Tap, Tap.

Yo!

Tap, Tap, Tap.

London! Open the door!

For what! I'm sleep and not in the mode for you or your bullshit!

Yo, hurry up! Man I almost got killed!

WHAT! Here I come!

Yo niggas was on shit tonight!

Why you say that and what happened? You sweating like crazy!

Man shit a nigga mouth was just reckless. He jive came at my man's sideways and I don't know why he felt the need to but he gathered up his crew. Shit! Niggas started exchanging words and before you knew it, niggas started drawing heat!

Wow! Well I'm glad no one was hurt.

Yeah me too! Oh and I'm sorry by the way.

Sorry about what?

For acting like I did, when you told me what was going on. I talked to Jazz and she told me you a really good girl. Plus my mom said to thank you for saying something because most bitches wouldn't.

Well that's the difference right there. I'm not a bitch!

Yeah you right! Plus I didn't realize how many females when I first came home from jail got these!

These what?

These nuts! Hahahaha!

Boy shut up!

Is you still taking your medicine?

Hell yeah, why would you ask me that question?

Well, because I brought a condom. You no good and well that I'm not about to be here in the same room with you and not tap that!

What!

You heard me!

Tapping is what got me in trouble in the first place. Not to mention did you take yourself to the doctor and get you fixed?

Hell yeah! My mom works for Sisters Medical Center.

Wow! Really!

Yeah really. Why you say it like that? What my mom can't have a job?

Nah it's not that, it's just Nye said her cousin saw. Nah! Never mind!

Saw what?

Nothing?

Saw what London?

Nevermind.

Let me tell you now! I don't do that gossip shit! Plus, some of your friends ain't really your friends anyway! Your little friend Sky be out every night. I'm surprised she don't tell you she see me out. The bitch always staring at me. I think she want these to.

These what?

These nuts!

Boy shut up! Sky is not like that. She would never do that to me.

Yeah okay! She a lil hot box! My man Bo said he hit it the same day he met her and she gave him the same shit we got!

They were at my mom's job together. I saw them when I went to get my medicine from my mom (Nasir felt relieved as London appeared to believe him).

Wow! Yeah okay! That explains it all. Whew!

What explains what?

Well Nye told me her cousin seen her with a guy that almost resembled you. I mean we had just discussed us, and then when I called her.

See stop putting your friends in our business. Didn't your mother ever tell you not to run your mouth, and what happens here stays here?

No!

Well, mines always told my sisters that! Hell she told them that so much I learned to live by the principle my damn self. You better learn that fucking with me! I'll be honest with you. I'm not your average kind of nigga. I come with shit. Either you accept me for who and all I am or let me know. I to have been hurt too, so that same shit you spit, applies here. I don't change easy, but willing for the right one. Now come and give me a kiss and quit playing. I know you see how hard you making my dick get. Teasing me with that tank top and panties on. Pop! (Sir smacks London's ass when she stands in front of him to provide the requested kiss).

That should not have happened!

So what are you saying?

Like seriously. You just seem to think you can do whatever you feel like doing whenever you feel like it!

What do you mean by that, and why do you feel the need to discuss it at 5:46 AM. I'm tired!

Well for one I haven't heard from you since I told you what was wrong with me. Secondly you decided to pop up over here unannounced at 4:00 AM, and thirdly.

Zzzzzz. Zzzzzzz

I know this nigga didn't fall asleep! Tuh!!!!!!!!!

Now this nigga knocked the hell out and I'm just laying here and shit. Bzzzzzz. bzzzzzz. bzzzzzzz. bzzzzzz. Fuck is that (London checks her phone)? bzzzzz. bzzzzz. bzzzzz. Oh this nigga done put his phone on vibrate, well he looked better just cutting the damn shit off. bzzzzz. bzzzzzz. bzzzzzz. What the? I know I'm not going to keep listening to this shit all night, well morning long.

He might be sleep for now, but we will continue this shit later!

bzzzzzz, bzzzzz, bzzzzz. Now I know I shouldn't be doing this, but somebody has a lot to fucking say early this morning. Only problem is (London sitting on the edge of her bed contemplating), how am I going to get this shit from under his arm without waking him up. Man forget it! I need to get some sleep anyhow. Mid-terms are tomorrow and I can't function without proper rest. On that note, fuck him and that phone!

Zzzzzzzz. Zzzzzzz. Zzzzzzzz.

Yo wake up! London, wake up!

What!

Wake up man. Is your kids here?

No why?

Cause I need to go to the bathroom and take a shit!

Too much information. You good. They come home today after school. Um, your phone was going off like crazy after you fell asleep on me to by the way. You might want to check it while you are on the toilet, if I may suggest.

Yeah I see it! It was text messages from my man. They got into some shit last night and was looking for me, that's all. Yo! Fuck I'm explaining myself to you for. You act like you pay my phone bill or something. I don't say shit to you when you be thinking you slick and cut the ringer off. You be sleep, while it's dark as hell. then all of a sudden, it start's lighting up and shit. Yeah I seen it, so what you have to say about your shit my dear? Right! Nothing! Cat must have your tongue. Ha!

I was just telling you as it could have been important!

If you felt that way about it, then why you let me keep sleeping? Listen one things for certain, and two things for sure. I don't owe you any explanations for anything. This my phone and that's your phone. What you do with your phone is your business and what I do with mines is mine. Yo let me take a shit! please and thank you!

Yeah sure will, with your full a shit ass self. London rolls her eyes and walks back into the bedroom.

What you say?

I said sure will, because I have to take a shit myself!

Aye, can you drop me off at my cousin's house on your way to school, please?

Sure, but you need to be ready in 5 minutes.

I'm ready now!

Okay, now listen. Like right now what we doing is cool in all but I'm not going to keep being your little come through partner.

What you mean come through partner?

You heard me. I mean you can't seriously think or believe that I feel we're in a relationship at all. I mean really Nasir let's be honest.

First off call me Sir, and secondly I'm with you just about every damn night. I mean what the fuck London. What a nigga got to do write it across the fucking sky or something. You know I fuck with you. I bring you around my entire family and my niggas, like grow up. Shit we not in grammar school. Fuck you want me to do write a note and ask you would you be my girl circle yes or no. That's kid shit.

So basically what you implying is that we are in a relationship then?

Basically! So tell your little boyfriends stop fucking calling and texting you crazy ass hours in the night.

You to then!

Yup! Like London you do understand my phone is going to go off all times of the night. I'm a street nigga and street niggas do street nigga shit. That being said you know what that means without me having to say anything else.

Yea I do if that's really the case. Just know that I'm far from stupid, half crazy and I move in silence.

So what that mean? What I'm supposed to be scared or something cause I'm not.

What you should understand is that I can be a gangster to and I treat people the way they want to be treated. My mama didn't raise no fool!

Chapter Two

" It Could Be Love!"

What up (Nasir speaks to a friend while getting out of the car)?

What's really good blood? I see you with a new one now. She come with a nice whip too I see. Where you find her at?

Chill B! You know how I do!

Yeah, yeah I do. So what brings you over this way?

Man she had to go to school and I ain't feel like sitting at my sister's house all day. Shit I got moves to make. I'll get with you though! Let me get my jack!

Ring, ring, ring.

Yo! Hey daddy, what's good with you? I miss you!

Who this?

Oh really papi! That's how you gon do me! It's Katina!

Aye, what up baby girl! Miss you too!

Oh do you?

Yeah I do.

Well when you coming to see me? I think I need my kitty kat scratched. Pur-r-r-r-r-r-r. Hahahahaha!

Girl you a mess. Ama see you though. You cooking?

For my Papi I will.

Okay, cool! Wait, hold on my other line clicking!

Hello!

Hey Sir! What's been up bae? Missing you!

Hey who dis?

Uh Meeka!

Oh hey bae what's up?

Nothing just was thinking about you.

Oh really!

Yes really!

Okay well what's good mama?

Well for starter's the fact that I didn't get my period this month!

Oh! So, what you want me to say about that? I'm not the doctor. Don't you think you should make yourself an appointment and see what the problem could be? Wait! Matter of fact, hold on!

Dang, what took you so long Papi?

Shit! Just had to handle some business baby, now back to what's most important.

Aww papi. Don't make me blush.

Ama do more than make you blush baby girl. Wash that pussy good, and tie your hair up. You know I love how when you bounce on this dick it falls straight down. Make sure my food hot too. No pork and I'll see you in about an hour or two.

Okay Papi! I'll be waiting for you!

************** Meanwhile on the block **************

Sheeka what you doing?

Blowing smoke dis, Sir?

Yeah, who the fuck you thought it was?

Nigga please! What you trying to chill and smoke?

Yeah come pick me up on Ferry in the bricks! meet me at the store across the street.

Okay be there in 5 and make sure you grab the dutches since you're at the store. I already have the smoke!

*********** Leaving from class ************

Ring, ring, ring!

Ring, ring, ring!

Hello!

Hey Sky, what's up with you?

Oh hey girl! I been meaning to call you. I've been so sick lately, it's been crazy.

Girl really!

Yes! Really! As a matter of fact, I had the same shit you had.

Damn! Like how likely is that, that two best friends/sisters could end up with the same dirty pussy disease at the same time. Ironic!

Yeah ironic, so you still talk to Nasir?

Yeah girl kinda why what's up?

Uh! Like why would you keep talking to a nigga that disrespected you when you came to him as a woman and told him what was wrong? Then to make matters worse, he went MIA on your ass for how long?

True but.

True but what? Like you stupid as hell London! That's why I keep it moving. These niggas ain't shit to be trusted. You really need to leave him alone. Nasir ain't shit!

Sky what the fuck is your problem? You seem to be way more, mad then me, and that's my nigga!

Yeah okay he yo nigga. From what it looks like he community property.

Fuck you mean what it looks like?

Exactly what said. Problem is your exactly what his type love. You dumb when it comes to love, stay in the house to fucking much, and don't question shit he say or do! Yo I gotta go!

Click!

This bitch dumb as hell (Sky continues to rant)! Couldn't be me! Shit I was mad after I fucked the nigga. Dick ain't even all that! I know one things for sure, I damn sure won't be having this baby! Shit how could I? I really need to stop drinking and letting my feelings get the best of me. I damn sure don't even know who the daddy could be. That's my fault lesson learned though. I'll be making my appointment pronto!

*********** Some Where Out There! ***********

Sheeka pass me that!

Here!

This some good shit right here. Sheeka where you get this from?

Goodyear!

Damn this loud got me higher than a piff!

What the fuck is a piff nigga!

Hahahahaha! Told you it got me higher than a Piff. Shit I don't even know what a piff is my damn self! Some shit I just made up!

You funny as hell nigga! Zip-p-p-p-p!

Wooooo! What you doing Sheeka?

Slurrrrrp!

Damn! Oh shit, that feels good!

Well you looked like you was having a rough day, so I thought I'd top you off!

Shit! I know you don't think I'm not about to hit!

Nope, I know you about to hit, that's why I sucked it like I did!

Yo hand me that gold wrapper, and bend it over!

Let me put it on for you.

Oh you wanna do that for daddy huh!

Nigga you ain't daddy, but yeah I'll do it for you!

Shit Sheek! You had to use yo mouth to do that too huh? You must really want this dick up inside of you. Bend it over and spread it! I'm up in that shit!

Hurry up, my nigga get off work soon!

Both Nasir and Sheeka had a great time. Neither wanted a relationship, while sadly this was just the type of friendship they had. Once they were done fucking, shit just seemed to go as if, what just happened never took place.

Sheek drop me off on the Westside yo! I got this move to bust.

Alright! Let me hop in the shower real quick as I have to go pick his lame ass up from work anyhow!

You know you the main reason why I don't trust bitches now. Yal come with all kinds of shit just to get with another nigga. Oh bae... I'm working overtime. Me and the girls going out. It's ladies night! My peoples in the hospital I be right back. Or I'm going out of town with my family. Someone died. Bitch please. I bet yo nigga gone be tight when he get home too. My dick done been all over that body and that's a fact!

Well since you know so much why don't you join me in here so that I can wash your back.

Told you bitches ain't shit!

Nasir takes his time getting re-dressed. As he reaches down to put

51

on his "Air Force One's" his mind wonders. Damn I really am a doggish nigga. London don't deserve me, but I want her. I really need to stop putting myself in these good for nothing ass situations. When I get my shit together I swear I'll do better by her. Damn! His head drops down and an eyebrow raises.

Yo Sheeka! Let's go. Play times over. We out!

Sir is definitely a mess with his doggish ways, but for some strange reason the women love him!

Knock. Knock. Knock. Yo!

Is that my papi?

What you thought girl! Open up!

Yesssssssss it is! Hi papi! Oh how I missed you! You smell that shit? I cooked what I know you would like. Oh and look at me papi! You see this (Katina smacks her ass)! It was waiting just for you.

Man baby girl. Papi is sorry, but papi don't feel good. Papi needs to lay down and tap a nap. I'm not gone be here to long anyhow. I got moves to bust!

listen! I Don't care about all your lame ass excuses. You told me you miss me and to cook for you! I told you that my kitty kat needed to be scratched and you agreed. Now whatever it was that had you changing your mind is pissing me off!

Listen baby! I did not come all the way over here for you to nag me and keep talking this fuck shit. Now I'm hungry as hell and wanna lay down. Can I do that? Damn! Let a nigga live. Shit! Soon as I walk in the door you throwing me pussy. That shit ain't cute. I could see if you was my bitch, but you probably doing the same shit too and with the next nigga. Fuck outta here with that shit ma'mi!

Oh so now you a tough Tony! Listen. You ruined my day and frankly your right I'm not your bitch! Here take this plate so I don't waste my food and get the fuck out of here!

Bitch what you say?

Oh you heard me Sir! A real bitch is not about to play with you. I sincerely respect myself more than this. You come in my home like you a boss and then try and talk shit to me. I'm not the one! No hard feelings but niggas want to fuck with me, so bye! Shit all you good for is me riding your face anyway!

Oh bitch now you tuff when you was just begging me to come through! You know what though! Ama do just what you said and leave. Don't hit my jack no more either (Sir grabs his plate and walks out slamming the door).

Now walking to the corner store Nasir realizes he needs to get a ride. Not sure of who may or may not be available he reaches in his pocket and pulls out his phone to make a call.

Ring, ring, ring,

What's up?

Fuck you mean what's up! Bitch come pick me up. I'm on the corner of Grant and Ferry.

(Sky pulls up) So who do you really think you are? Like you think you some Godly ass nigga don't you?

Sky shut the fuck up! You the dirty bitch so own it! Here it is you out here fucking mad niggas and not only mad niggas but your friend's niggas too! Now don't get all hush hush now with your infected ass pussy!

Where the fuck am I dropping you off at? I don't even know why I even entertained the thought of picking you up!

Yeah I bet you don't know. In all honesty you a mad bitch! All you keep doing secretly is comparing yourself as to why I didn't chose you. On some real shit I like London. I may not show it but baby girl alright!

Well if you like her so much why you in the car with me?

What part didn't you get? I-needed-a-ride! Simple! I mean you couldn't have though for one second that I would really want to fuck with a bitch that's recklessly easy, and who shits on her teammates. Nah that ain't me boo. Hell if you could cross her for some dick, I could only imagine what money would do.

Oh don't try and preach to me. You just as wrong and you know what? Since you in my car with your walking ass, why don't we go keep it real with your girl, since you fake claiming her!

Sky drives close to London's house purposely. She had every intent to see if this nigga was really feeling London. She was jealous, but would never directly admit it. Sky had amazing green colored eyes, only wore bundles because she wanted too, her shape was that of a perfect coca cola bottle, and her smile was to die for. Sky never had a problem with a man, and Nasir was by far her first!

Ring. Ring. Ring.

Hello!

Hey girl what's up?

Who is this?

It's Nye! Why did I just see Sir getting out of your car at the gas station?

Bitch you tripping! Like seriously do you know how many bitches is riding around Buffalo, NY with an Impala? I do not now or ever have time for this type of drama! It's already bad enough I have enough on my plate and your simple ass just gone call me and accuse me of some dumb shit like that! Damn you worse than a nigga. Stop ridding my heels please!

Who you think you talking too? You got the game fucked up! That's what I do know. I wouldn't stalk your hoeish, stank pussy, fucking everybody else man in the first place for one. With the way you talking you guilty as fuck anyhow. My mama taught me to trust my intuitions and I highly doubt they wrong!

Nye would you please shut the fuck up! Bitch you fucking just as many niggas as me. The only dumb one is London stupid ass for always falling in love trying to be all wifed up and shit! She the only one living in La-la land.

Sky you dirty and I don't give a fuck if I'm fucking your father. Wrong is wrong and right is right. That's my friend hell more like a sister and I'm going to tell her just what I saw.

So you just gonna go and start some shit huh! Well if you saw him getting out of my car why yo dumb ass ain't offer him a ride? Matter of fact while you wasting your time talking to me, I'm sure he still walking go and get him CLICK!

She better hope, wish and pray that this ain't true. I swear on everything I love I would beat the breaks that bitch for my girl.

Knock. Knock. Knock. Yo!

Yo what? Like listen, you can't keep just popping up over here all ghetto rude, and shit! My Kids are sleeping as they have school in the morning and I have a class myself.

Shut yo ass up girl. I missed you!

You missed me huh? Well that is extremely hard to tell considering you hadn't called or texted me since I dropped you off this morning.

Damn girl you nag but I jive like that shit! How was your day?

It was okay, and thanks for asking. How was yours?

Great. Do I have any clean under clothes here? I need to take a shower yo. My body hurt bad as hell too. You feel like rubbing my back for me when I get out the shower?

Sure why not, but let me just make sure the kids sleep first.

Damn I love this girl and she don't even know it!

Ding dong! Ding dong! London's doorbell suddenly begins to ring, causing a shocked expression to appear on her face. Nasir wrinkled up his nose and began to think about all the devious shit he has been engaging in.

Yo! Who the fuck is that?

Uhhh I don't know; however, I'm about to find out. At least they aint yelling Yo and knocking on my door like the police!

Hey girl! I'm sorry to come by so late but you got a minute?

Yeah girl come in what's up?

Well. Wait! Who here with you?

What! Girl you know that's Sir! Who else would it be?

Oh! Uhhhh!

What Nye? Fuck all that uhhhh stuff. It's late and as I just told you I have company.

Well girl I don't think Sky or Nasir is any good for you!

What makes you say that?

Let's just say I seen them together just minutes before I arrived. Now grant it I should of called but I called Sky first to get an idea of what was going on. Now had she just been giving him a ride I could have understood. Considering her behavior while on the phone that was a red flag.

Red flag huh! That's funny you say that as she raised my eyebrow when I talked to her earlier.

You talked to Sky earlier?

Yea!

That bitch ain't shit!

Nye calm down. Let's check into this first before blaming anyone about something we just feel is wrong. I thank you for keeping it real and ama holler at you later.

Okay girl! Love ya! Bye! And just be careful with this clown!

London attempts to walk back to her room calm, but it's killing her putting all the event's in order. As much as she doesn't want to believe what she is processing her intuition is speaking loudly.

No wonder this bitch was acting funny. Hmmm! This nigga ain't even no better, but that fact that she was calling me sis and we was extra tight pisses me off even more!

58

Zzzzzzz. Zzzzzzzzz. Zzzzzzzz.

Oh I see he put his phone on vibrate again. Huh! Enough is enough.

Knock. Knock. Knock.

What's up baby girl, you wanna come in?

No bae! I was just seeing how much longer you were going to be. You know I have school tomorrow and I'm ready to lay down.

****London scrolls threw Sirs text messages****

Alright. Just give me 10 mins. Make sure you butt ass naked when I come out too!

Okay! Will do. London responds sarcastically allowing her enough time to continue snooping around.

Message 1: you just gonna keep ignoring me huh! You know you want me!

Message 2: Hey boo lol wyd

Message 3: Sir u coming up in me opps you coming to see me I mean. Lol

Message 4: You wasn't saying all that when you was eating my pussy and fucking me nigga! You said you wanted me anyhow in the first place. You was only being nice cause yo man liked me.

Message 5: I put yo medicine in yo sisters mailbox BITCH! I hate you

Message 6: Idk why you mad at me when we both was wrong. You mad at me and after we fucked 4 times and I gave you head. It's not fair. You should have kept it honest and real with me.

Reply to message 6 from Sir: What do you mean about keeping it real. You a fake ass friend and ama tell my girl about you my damn self, watch!

Oh these mother fuckers got me twisted.

Bae! Take my lotion out. I'm on my way!

Meanwhile Nye is just out in the street's riding around. The mere sight of Nasir and Sky together kept playing in the back of her mind. Nye begins to speak out loud to herself.

Something just doesn't feel right. I already don't like this Sir character so to even have my so-called friend involved makes matters worse. I wasn't feeling our conversation with ole-girl earlier either. Matter of fact! Let me slide by there. Need to see this bitch facial expression when we talk.

Knock. Knock. Knock.

Wait a minute here I come.

Hello, who is it?

Nye!

What the fuck! Why are you here? Do you have any sense of what time it is. What you took my advice and gave Sir a ride or something? Sky starts to giggle. Wait let me guess you went over London's to tell and he was already there blocking!

Well if you must know I did and there was no blocking being done at all. Now are you going to open this door or what?

The door suddenly opens.

Like I thought!

Bitch who do you think you are? Like when did you start working for BPD. You a broke bitch and a clown. You stay playing yaself always asking for something from somebody now all of a sudden you barging over here trying to preach! FOH Nye! As a matter of fact. Get the fuck out!

You know what I will, and for the most part I was never a clown or punk and to prove it POP!

Bitch did you just hit me?

Bop, Pop, Bam, Slam! Bitch don't never try to play me. I'm sure yo mama taught you to respect yo elders. Stank pussy bitch. Smile for the camera!

Flash!

Nye takes a picture of Sky laid out on her mamas kitchen floor and leaves. Smiling but pissed at the same time for even having to witness a so-called friend be trifling. As much as Nye knew this would hurt London, she was prepared and ready to show her why.

Who the fuck she think she is? Like really. It's going to take Jesus and all of his apostles to get me to talk to her again!

Bae! How long do you think you will be?

London I'm in the shower and if you stop bothering me, maybe I could get out sooner.

This nigga think he slick, but he don't even know. London still scrolling through his phone, until. Ring. Ring. Ring. Hello!

What's up girl what you doing?

Who's this?

Mary!

Oh okay girl, not much! Nah am lying I'm pissed.

Pissed about what?

Well Nye came through to tell me she saw Sir with Sky and it didn't look good!

You heard from him?

Yeah he in the shower now! And to make matters worse, I know I shouldn't have done this but I just looked in his phone.

Well what you see?

Let me read them to you Mary. I Have to hurry up, because I told you he was here.

Message 1: Hey Nasir how's your day? If you not too busy hmu!

Message 2: So was it everything you thought it could be? Told you, you should have picked ME!

Message 3: WYD

Message 4: Hey what's up?

Message 5: Word so you just going to keep ignoring my text huh? You a clown ass nigga anyway. You hit and now you MIA! Foh

Message 6: Oh so it's just my fault you got that shit huh? You knew what time it was when you slide up in this pussy. You just as dirty. Lord only knows how many bitches you done fucked.

Message 7: So you choosing well fuck you and London's raggedy ann looking ass. Just wait till I drop the dime!

WHAT!!!!! Okay wait! Mu-Sah! Who the fuck do this bitch think she is? She got some nerve fucking behind you first. Secondly trying to steal yo man and thirdly mad as hell trying to dis both of you after he told her he was fucking with you! That bitch need her ass whopped!

like I know right! I'm mad as hell. What really pisses me off is.....

Yo can you hand me my tooth brush off the dresser
Wait hold on Mary. Okay! What pisses me off is that she threatens

to tell me on him like I was going to respect the shit that she did anyways!

Girl listen! You need to put that nigga the fuck out of yo house and go whip that bitch ass. Matter of fact bitch, put yo clothes on. Tell that nigga you got business to take care of. I'm on my way!

Oh my God Mary no! I can't tonight. I swear we can handle this tomorrow with Sky. I have to deal with him tonight myself. You know what they say is always right. "Trust your intuitions" and " You get what you looking for".

Yeah well that may be so, but he still need to get the fuck out. Both are dirty as hell. Call me if you need me!

Click!

That shower was good as hell bae! You would have thought a nigga didn't shower in a week. Nasir walks out the bathroom with a towel wrapped around his husky waits, another laying across his shoulders while using yet a third one to dry his head. What's wrong with you?

What's wrong with me? Listen, I'm no longer going to hold it in. I know you got that stank pussy disease from Sky! You nasty and foul and so is she. For that reason alone, I'm done with you and her so do yaself the honor of drying off, getting dressed, packing ya shit and getting the hell out of here!

So what you mad? Can you handle the truth? If you want me to go I will. This right here is one of the main reasons why niggas lie!

Listen that night we met, your girl was all on me. She kept staring. She stayed throwing hints at me, and she went as far as to slip her number in my jacket pocket with a note. I still have it. I knew what I was doing was wrong but shit she kept coming for me. I gave her the dick yup I sure did, but I also told that bitch numerous times, she couldn't steal the kid. It seemed to me the more I told her I wanted you, the more she would harass me. Seriously. I told her I was going to come clean ad tell you. Hell I tried numerous times.

You telling me the truth has absolutely everything to do with how my feelings are being displayed. What because you told me the truth I'm just supposed to not care! I'm hurt! Like the one person I trusted crossed me and who's to say if another bitch cross me you won't be willing to experiment with her as well. This whole situation is fucked up and I don't know how to feel right now, I really don't.

Listen! How many times do I have to tell you that I don't have to be here! Like what part of that you don't understand! I ain't have to tell you shit and I didn't have to make you my girl.

You right about everything you just said. So do what you feel you have to. You and Sky both ain't shit and with that potty ass mouth of yours you can kiss my ass! Wait you already did that. Like I don't know who the fuck you think you talking to, but I'm far from these bitches you seem to enjoy!

Yo hand me my shit! I'm the fuck up out of here!

"Bye Craig" " You ain't gotta lie Craig" London says while jokingly referencing a line from one of her favorite movies.

She attempts to throw Nasir his pants and sweatshirt at him in the process.

Stop grabbing me! Move!

I'm sorry! Stop playing you know you love me!

Get off of me! I thought I knew you until today! Move! Stop! No! Wait! No! Yesssssss! Right there! Ummmmmm! You win tonight, but you are out of here in the morning!

Hahahaha SLURP! Ahhhhhhh! I'm not… slurp! Going… slurp! No… slurp! Where! Slurpppppppp with a wicked tongue wiggle!

Sir was nasty and he knew it. London knew it too and had a crazy attraction to that shit as well. She was a lady in the streets and a definite freak in the bedroom. Hands down Sir knew it too, and that's why he kept baby girl close.

You make me sick! I hope you know that right?

Nah! You love me and this (sir sticks his tongue out and wiggles it).

You really are crazy. You hungry?

I sure am! Matter of fact. Some French toast, cheese eggs, grits and fried potato's would be nice, but you probably not about that life.

What you mean? Boy please! Let me go brush my teeth and do the sign of the cross. I'll be right back!

Zzzzzzz. Zzzzzzzz. Zzzzzzz.(Sir phone begins to vibrate).

Bae where you going?

Zzzzzzzz.zzzzzzz.zzzzzzz.

I'll be right back!

716-253-3231Ringgggg. Ringgggg.

Hello!

What up?

Hey Boo! What's been going on? I haven't heard from you!

Word! Awww. What you miss me or something?

You know that!

Well unfortunately babe, I don't miss you! Not trying to sound mean or hurt yo feelings, but if you hadn't heard from me by now what in the hell would make you think I want to be bothered. I just answered my phone to tell you I'm good. Please stop hitting me up as my girl would be mad!

WHAT! Nigga don't think you can talk to me any fucking way. All you had to say is that you didn't want me calling instead of leading me on. Like fuck you!

Hahahaha! You mad huh?

Not as mad as your bitch is going to be when I see yal. You better warn her! Click!

*** 6 weeks later ***

Hello London! Glad you could make it in today. The doctor will be in too see you shortly. In the meantime let me get your weight and vitals. Everything looks good and Doctor will be right in!

She lucky I love her and shit. Got me up in the clinic to make sure my dick right. Who she think she is yo! Hell my nasty ass haven't even been cheating this time. Bet he tell me something wrong she gone have some fucking explaining to do!

Nasir West!

Yes

Come in please!

Okay London. If you could just relax. Now you may feel a little pressure as I look in here; however, you just relax and breath.

Okay!

So far everything looks good. I'll send the cultures over to lab and let you know if there is anything wrong. You may get dressed.

Do you have any questions for me?

Yes! So that discharge I'm having is normal?

From what it looks like yes. There aren't any symptoms appearing that are causing me any real concerns at this time. It appears that you may either be in ovulation or just experiencing a hormone adjustment. Let me review everything then we can both be certain.

Hello Mr. West! It's a pleasure to meet you today. How may we help you?

Ummm Hhhhhi Doctor! Ughhhh my girl want me to get checked out! Like a physical I guess.

Hahahaha! Okay! I'm sure I know exactly what kind of physical you need. Well what we are going to offer you first and is in no parts mandatory is to get checked out for the HIV virus.

What! Ummmm. Okay! I guess.

No worries and it will be rather quick. After the nurse comes in to draw your blood and take your vitals I'll make sure everything is in good condition.

Sir sat patiently awaiting the doctor's to come back in the room, while London was in a room a few doors down.

Well London. As I told you there wasn't much to worry about; however, there is something going on that brings a little concern to me.

What Doctor? What is it?

How have you been feeling honestly?

Fine Doctor! Seriously. Why would you ask? Is there something wrong?

Your weight seriously has declined. You have lost 10 pounds since the last time we saw you. Are you having complications eating. Is there anything stressful in your life?

No Doctor! Not that I'm aware of!

Well London from what the test project. Your Pregnant! This type of weight loss isn't good for you or a new fetus. As You know your periods are extremely irregular so I am going to schedule you for a sonogram immediately!

Sir wasn't very good at cleaning up his messes. While trying to live a new life and be faithful he intentionally hurt a lot of other women's feeing during the process.

Hey girl what up?

Cooling smoking on this hydro! What's good?

Listen! Some shit is going to have to go down and real soon.

What it do? Say shit not right, and you know we coming ready to fight! Who ass need that tap?

Well I don't know yet, but as soon as I do.

What you mean you don't know? G-code violation. Don't start no shit and don't know where it's going or who it's going to for that matter.

Listen! You remember the nigga Bresha hooked me up with?

What the nigga you was hooked up with in jail, and swore he was coming home to you. That when he got out, was paroled to his sisters and he told you she a church going person so you can't just be coming by without calling nigga? Yeah what about him?

Okay miss know it all. Yeah him! That mutha fucka gone tell me that he hasn't been calling me because he don't want to fuck with me no more. Nigga gone tell me he got a whole bitch and shit! Not to mention I put that nigga on and let him attempt to flip a $1000.00 of my taxes and didn't even get mad when he fucked it up!

Yeah well that's yo shit! You the fool for that! I love you and I fuck with you but I'm not about to brick no bitch fa that!

Yeah well that nigga and whoever he with is going to get it! I gave up a year of my life paying comminsary, putting money on my phone constantly, paying for him to have food. Letting him get out and let his baby mama shit on him so It could be me as his main bitch to only get played! Not to mention bitch Im pregnant and called to tell him that! Fuck outta here!

Well it's on then! Get at me when you got info!

I will and thank you!

Now this young lady was upset. She helped him do his time and he wasted no time letting her know it just wasn't going to work out. She played her position so she thought hoping that she would be picked, but when that all back-fired she was tight. Now she's pregnant and looking for revenge. Be-careful London!

************ Nasir & London leaving the Doctor **********

Now that that's over you want something to eat baby girl?

Yeah why not?

What's wrong with you? Is there something I should know? What the doctor say to you in there, cause you have a whole attitude now!

Sir I'm pregnant!

What? For real? London don't lie to me!

Yes Nasir I am, but there are some concerns.

Like what?

Well the doctor for one is going to send me for a sonogram tomorrow. This is to determine how long/far I may be. I don't menstruate regularly so it's hard to predict when I conceived. Then he feels I have too much stress on me as my weight is not what he feels safe to begin a pregnancy with. So I guess I'm a little down. My body has never been the most healthy and pregnancies have always been my biggest struggle.

Baby don't worry. *Zzzzzzz. Zzzzzzz. Zzzzzzz.* (Sir looks at his phone real quick) We got this! We need to get you and my lil baby something to eat and then get you home to sleep. I Love you girl! I really hope you know that!

Zzzzzzz. Zzzzzzz. Zzzzzzz. (Sir looks at his phone again).

Zzzzzzz. Zzzzzzzzz. Zzzzzzz.

I see you real important today!

London don't start with me. You know I be having to make moves.

Yeah but from the look on your face that was far from a move.

Damn ma! You eyeing me like that! Come on now. We having a good day. Don't start no shit it won't be no shit okay?

Okay! Well where we going because I could go for some chicken fingers. Honey mustard with fries and a side of cheddar cheese, barbeque sauce and an extra blue cheese! Ummmm. Oh and a cola!

Damn girl okay! Shit we gone go to my peoples spot. Oh and you gone have to pay for it cause I don't have no money on me right now okay?

But you making moves. Here! (London hands him a twenty dollar bill) and I want my money back!

I got you. Go ahead and order it. Just get me a quarter pound double with no tomato, a strawberry milkshake and fries.

Zzzzzzz. Zzzzzzz. Zzzzzzzz.

Zzzzzzz. Zzzzzzzz. Zzzzzzzz.

******* Sir goes to the men's room to read his messages*******

Message 1 from Brikinna.
Yeah okay mutha fucka. Guess What? I'm pregnant and 2.5 months to be exact. I won't be having an abortion so if I were you, you better let lil girl know!

Message 2 from Sissy
Yo it's too many bitches just popping up at my house looking for you unannounced. This shit has to chill immediately or you're going to have to find somewhere else to live!

Message 3 from Brikinna
Oh and when I find out who ole girl is......she's done! You should know how I get down by now!!!!

Sir makes a prompt decision to all call Brikinna due to the threat she just texted. He is now pissed and after what happened the last time to London when she was pregnant, he was not about to take any chances.

Yo listen here! If anything and I do mean anything should happen to my girl bitch you and that bastard ass baby you trying to blame on me is done! Bitch we ran a whole train on yo dumb molly popping ass and you thought I was choosing you! Dumb bitch stop calling me I'm good!!!

As Nasir walks out of the bathroom he takes note to London balled up in her booth seat with waitresses surrounding her.

What's wrong yo?

My stomach hurts. It hurts really bad!

Okay! Ummmm. Okay! Ughhhh what you want me to call yo doctor or take you to the hospital? Wait, better yet, I can call my sister.

Jasintra is no fucking doctor. That's my sis too but what is her coming over here going to do? Like really!

Okay! I guess you right. Well what you want me to do? I'm nervous.

Take me to the hospital. This shit is only getting worse.

Sir if I may interrupt one of the waitresses says. I think we should call 911. I'm sure that you would rather her be safe than sorry. She told us she just found out she was having a baby. We should really call 911.

Okay, your right. I'll follow the ambulance to the hospital when they get here. Bae is there anyone else I should call.

No, not right now. I just want to see what's wrong first.

Welcome to Sisters of Medical Service Center.

Before you sign in, please make sure you have your New York State ID and Insurance information. Now what brings you here today?

Nurse my stomach started cramping, and it seems as though it only got worse after I was throwing-up.

Over to the side in the public waiting room two girls continuously stare at whisper. Hey is that Nasir with some bitch over there? Ooooooooh girl yes it is! Damn what would Shameria say if she knew about this. I bet she would be shitting bricks, Girl I don't even know! Didn't she say he was supposed to be out of town shooting some music video? Sure did! Girl take a picture and call her. You know she don't believe shit unless you got proof.

Well maybe we should wait because we don't know who ole girl is. She could be family. Yeah well from the way he holding her up, she far from family! Yeah but we should still wait. Flash! Too bad as I took the picture just in case anyways.

Good news for the both of you! From the looks of everything, everything is all good. Now what you will need to do is up your water intake!

Told you about drinking all that pop!

Hahaha! That's good to know. Water not Soda dear. Also you will be on bed rest for 2 weeks then follow up with your regular OBGYN. When she is sleeping try placing pillows under her feet and not saying you are, but limiting stress would be suggested at this time. Are there any questions?

No doctor will do. Are we clear to go home now?

Yes but before you leave out pick up a prescription from the nurses station. These are additional vitamin supplements to help strengthen your body. As you get older pregnancies get more complicated. Congratulations and make sure you follow up in 2 weeks!

Thank you!

See bae, I told you about drinking all that dark pop. As soon as we leave I'm going to get you some juice and water. A voice calls out from across the room. H-e-e-e-e-y Sir! So this the video you shooting huh? Bitch get the fuck out my face. Come on London fuck these thugly bitches!

Thugly! You wasn't saying that when your head was buried in this thugly pussy.

Sir what the fuck?

Bitch shut the fuck up! What he gave you some shit cause he good for it. Ole dirty dick mutha fucka! Matter of fact how about I Just Beat that bitch ass! Sir instantly grabs London and begins to fight with Shameika. While Sir has Shameika pinned up with a bloody nose her friends begin to jump London!

Hit the alert button now!

Instantly police come running in the waiting room bursting open doors screaming! You have the right to remain silent! Anything you say can and will be held against you!

Wait says one of the nurses at the desk. Officers, I believe you are making a drastic mistake. Grant it this young man put his hands on that woman, but she and her entire crew came here deliberately with intent to cause harm and endanger the life of a pregnant woman.

Radio ten-four please send back up cars immediately. We have three additional suspects who could be charged with assault and attempted murder and/or endangerment. The suspect harmed was/is pregnant!

Oh my God! Why didn't you say that girl was pregnant. The suspects attempt to have a small conversation while being cuffed to the bench. I'm not going to jail for no foolery. I tell you that!

Call it what you want but I didn't know that bitch was pregnant!

You got us in a boat load of shit over this clown ass fake wanna be the shit ass nigga.

Bitch you try me and see where it gets you. Now if I'm not mistaken you screen shot me! Not only do I have the picture, but the text to prove it. I didn't ask you or your little bald headed ass friend to help me. You jumped in all on your own.

Ladies! You have the right to remain silent! Anything you say can and will be held against you. You will be entitled to one call when we arrive at booking headquarters. Is there anyone here other than yourselves who can be responsible for your property such as a vehicle. If so the nurse station can generate a page.

78

Code blue ER room #16
Code blue ER room #16

While at their grandmothers Siyion and Sincere begin to question where there mother is. London was never the kind to leave her kids unattended or somewhere unsafe. Nine times out of ten they were with her mom. It was unlikely for them not to hear from her by now and they both were concerned.

Where's mommy Siyion?

I don't know She didn't answer her phone.

Well you think you should tell granny to pick us back up?

Listen! I got you! Mommy don't need all those problems. Remember what daddy put her through? It took mommy a long time to snap out of that. She was really hurt.

Yeah brother I know. I just wish we had the mommy back that was happy and did things with us like she used too.

Yeah me to Siy. I don't know what this man is doing but it seems like he only wants her. I don't even think he wants us around. That man barely even speaks when I see him. As much as I don't like it, I try and find a positive way to look at things. Just by doing that Maybe mommy will see and things will get better. It's getting late. Good night Brother! Good night Sister!

Siyion makes sure his sister is in bed, before he walks in his room and kneels down to pray. Lord I lay me down to sleep. I should die before I awake, I pray to you Lord my soul to take. God bless my mommy, my sister, my granny and my grand pa. Please Lord make sure my mommy is alright. I won't ask for anything for Christmas if you would just make sure she came home safe and without him!

Amen!

While leaving the hospital Nye attempts to comfort London. After Sin getting hauled off to jail, and yet again having a confrontation with yet another one of Nasir's hoes she breaks down.

London girl it's gonna be alright! Give me your keys. You just sit in the car. I'll go in and check on the kids, take your stuff in the house and then come back and get you.

As much as she tried to dry her eyes she just couldn't. The pain and hurt of the situation was tearing at her deeply. Crazy as it seemed, but her husband's ex-husband that is face keep appearing in her head. This only made matters worse.

Mommy! Is that you? Hey Siyion it's auntie Nye! Hey where's my mom? She's in the car. She wasn't feeling good. I believe she had food poisoning. I'm about to bring her in now. Do me a favor and pull her cover back for me, okay?

Okay! Siyion is excited to see his mom and be helpful to her. Although he hadn't not a clue what food poisoning was, all he was concerned with was his mom being home. Oh without him!

Look girl. Siyion is up! Fix your face. I told him you weren't feeling good and that you had food poisoning. Oh okay! Wait! Where's my phone? I got it! It's in your hospital bag with your other belongings. I wonder if Sir called yet. Aren't they given a call as soon as they get booked? Yes they do. I wonder how he is going to feel when I tell him I lost the baby!

Well not meaning to sound or be rude but now wasn't a good time for you to have a baby any way. Look we about to go in and remember you had food poisoning.

MOMMY! Both kids yelled while running up to hug her. Mommy Siyion is the best brother. I'm not going to lie mommy because that is bad but I was scared you left us and didn't love us anymore! Siyion reaches over and pinches his sister. Ouch! What you do that fir stupid! Hahaha, well mommy loves you both. London bends down and hugs and kisses them both. Mommy isn't feeling well so I'm going to lay down. It's bed time for you both as you have school in the morning. Get back in the bed and maybe we will go and get ice cream tomorrow! Nye interrupts, Yeah and I'm spending the night so I'll be the one taking you both to school tomorrow.

Awwww mannnnn. Both kids speak in unison. Nye looked strange to the response from both her favorite niece and nephew.

Good night mommy and we love you.

Get better mommy and I won't be scared no more!

Suddenly the phone rings. Hello! You have a collect call from an inmate in the Erie County holding center. To accept press 2. Beep

Hey baby what happened?

Fuck you mean what happened London! I'm in jail. What you

didn't think I was going to let them bitches just jump you and my baby did you? Did you? You hear me, Did you?

Feeling the hurt of the entire situation all over again London begins to cry. Bae we loss the baby!

Ughhhhhhhhhhh! What! Them bitches gonna get everything they deserve bae okay! I swear that everything is going to be alright! I'm sorry man I'm so fucking sorry and I mean it! The judge gave them bitches 90 days but ama have something waiting on that ass when they come out!

No bae that's not what I want or need. We will be fine I promise you. This shit hurts but I'll be fine.

Yeah okay bae but them bitches still gone get it. Do me a favor okay! Go get a pen and paper.

Got it!

Call my mom Mrs. Dean and tell her my bail is 2500. She gonna give you 2000 and I need you to put in just the 500 for me till I get out. As soon as I get home I'll reimburse you okay?

(long pause) O-k-a-y

London does exactly what Sir ask of her. Although she was hesitant she still provided the money as requested. Being on bed rest she was unable to attend court with his mom, so she awaited his mother's call to inform her of his release.

************** Meanwhile ***************

Ringgggggg. Ringgggggg. Ringgggggg.

Hello?

London!

Hey mommy what's up?

You Tell me! Siyion tells me that the one pair of sneakers his no good ass father finally purchased him are missing. He didn't want to tell you, because he said you wouldn't believe him. Why he feels like that I don't know which is why I'm calling to ask you. Well in being honest mommy I don't know. As you know I've been a bit under the weather.

Yo! I know you not still laying the fuck around in this dirty ass house, Nasir yells out as he walks in completely unannounced. Like do you ever make yo kids clean up after they self. How the fuck you just lying in the bed probably talking to one of yo corny ass friends, not talking about shit. Funny how you couldn't show up with my mom like I asked you too. Them bitches need a man of they own, while they always trying to tell you something about me. Tell them bitches to SUCK MY DICK! hahahahaha.

Who the fuck is that over there London? Huh? Who is he telling to suck his little penis. You better tell that mutherfucker who the hell I am, if you have any sense. No wonder Siyion and Sincere haven't been wanting to come back home. I tell you this! Anything and I do mean anything happens to my grandchildren, shit is going to get really real. CLICK!

Mom!

Oh you was talking to yo mother? Opps oh well. Shit if she ain't like what I had to say she can suck my dick too for all I care.

Oh my God! You really need to chill. That was my mother I was talking to and you completely didn't make a good first impression.

Impression! Hahaha. Girl bye! Either she's going to respect a real nigga or she's not. Shit what I say wrong? You laying the fuck in the bed like you can't get your life back in order. Grant it, you lost the baby, but that was about a week ago! Dishes piled up in the sink. Bathroom dirty as hell. Shit all in the front-room. Like! You a grown ass woman who act more like a kid. Get yo shit in order. As far as I'm concerned. You can't say shit to me. Hell you can't even check yo kids. Fuck outta here!

What you mean? You grown, and I don't see you helping do shit here either!

Why should I? This ain't my house! This you, yo kids, and yo mama shit. Ya heard! Hell them ain't even my kids and you want me to clean up after them. Right! Picture that! Where the keys at yo? I got shit to do.

Yeah okay shit to do huh. You think I'm stupid. Who is she Sir? Huh! Who is she? You was just all in love now you want to argue and look for excuses to validate the shit you out here doing.

Girl I don't need validation. I'm a valid nigga. You should be
happy I'm even staying here right now. No worries cause honestly
it's only temporary. As soon as I get my shit together I'm gone. I
didn't want to come here no way. You were just my best move at
the time and you wanted me here. Remember when you first asked
me I told you no!

You know what Sir. You're really mean, and what's funny is you
do wear the same size sneaker as my son and now all of a sudden
his shit coming up missing. Yeah let me find out your valid broke
ass stole my son shit.

Bitch! Don't you never in yo life accuse me of some wack ass shit
like that. Wait! You know what! Get your lazy ass up and take me
to my mothers. I'm not staying here no more and nor am I fucking
with you. It's a wrap yo! You to childish and stupid for me!

And they say God works in mysterious ways! If I've never been
more happy I lost a kid, I'm excited as hell. How dare you come at
me talking about my shit when you ain't even have a room where
you were staying. Now all of a sudden you can go to yo mama's!
Well I tell you what have her pick yo don't have shit in life, but 3
garbage bags ass up. You talking so much shit and don't even have
a window to throw it out of!

Ohhhh hahaha! Now you got balls. Well I see why yo husband
ain't want yo ass and had a baby on you. Shit from the looks of it
you can't even have kids no way. You a fucking bug a boo. All you
do is nag wine and cry. Grow up! Matter of fact you don't have to
take me nowhere. I never needed you for shit anyhow. My girl will
come get me with no problem.

Hell she cook better then you, clean up better than you and take care of her kids better then you. Ha she could probably have a baby better then you!

GET OUT! (glass breaks as London throws her cup)

Hahahaa. You mad now right? Get yo shit in order and maybe I'll fuck back with you. As for now I'm outta here. Nasir dials a number on his phone and talks while in the bathroom. Hey come pick me up on the corner of Castle and Kensington. Don't bring nobody with you I have shit to put in the car. After hanging up the phone he continues speaking to London as he walks out the bathroom. Hopefully you, ya mother and ya kids happy now.

Chapter Three

" *Let The Games Begin!*"

Hello!

Hey Nye what's really good?

Who is this?

Hahahaha! I know we haven't talked in a while but you honestly forgot my voice?

All I'm saying is who is this?

Damn! Okay! It's Sky.

WHAT! Okay and what is it that brings you the audacity to call me almost a year later?

Well I wanted apologize to you and London. I knew that it wouldn't be possible without me getting in contact with you first.

Really?

Yes really. I've turned my life around and can only ask for forgiveness. I made a huge mistake and I'm trying to be woman enough to bring that to the table and repair what we shared before Nasir came and wrecked it.

Nasir? Wrecked it? I'm not sure who you trying to fool for one. For two you were her friend. We all know niggas ain't loyal or shit for that matter, but you fucked that man and tried to take him. Got that ass beat twice for being malicious or did we forget?

Well how are they doing anyhow if I may ask? Streets have it that they are no longer together.

Okay so what that mean?

Well I just was inquiring. Oh and if we could all settle our past differences I wanted to invite you both to my baby shower.

Baby shower? Who got you knocked the hell up?

Well that's also what I wanted to talk to you both about. I Made the choice myself to have this baby. Unfortunately I know that I wasn't shit and alcohol was having its way with my life. I' m a God fairing woman now and forgiveness is all I ask.

Bitch get to the point!

Well it is a strong possibility it could be Nasir's child as well as two other gentlemen. It all happened so quick! Please understand and don't judge me.

Bitch bye!

Nye now completely annoyed decides to get up and go grab a bite to eat, while London rest's asleep in her room at home.

Beep! (London receives a text message)
December 21st 2011. 3:48 am
Listen London I'm sorry! I never meant for things to go bad

between us. We were really cool and getting along.

Text #2 4:05 am
I know I said some hurtful things and put you through hell but seriously I need some help! I never told you but you are one of the only people who really care about me.

Text #3 4:28 am
I know I should have never put you through the things I did. Shit was hard for me growing up. My dad really wasn't shit if you ask me. Look at all the different mothers my brothers and sisters have.

Text #4 4:45am
I've been thinking about you a lot! It's killing me thinking about another man even having you in his possession. Shit sometimes when I'm sleeping. I can smell you. Silly right?

Text #5 5:08 am
I know your probably sleeping and when you awake and read these text you're probably going to say this nigga but yes this nigga!

Text #6 5:26 am
I love you London and I want you back! Please tell me what is it I have to do because whatever it is it's going to be done. I know you still love me how could you not?

Text #7 5:45 am
Remember we said to death do us part and I'm still living B! I love you and my kids and I hope it's not too late to make it right! Oh yeah and the nigga you with ain't shit, but you already know that I'm sure!

9:05 AM Mommy! Mommy! Wake up! Wake up mommy!

Okay, okay! I'm up! What am I late for something? Whats going on?

Look mommy! Daddy sent you these (1 dozen pink roses and 1 dozen white). He gave me and my brother some money too! Aren't you happy mommy! I prayed every night like you told me before bed. I knew God was going to hear me mommy. Daddy is going to save and protect us all. Watch mommy!

Ummm okay baby. Yes everything is nice and I will talk to him later!

Yayyyy Siyion! Mommy happy! Mommy happy!

(meanwhile) 716-425-3553. Ringggggg. Ringgggg. Ringgggg.

Hey baby good morning!

Good morning? What the fuck are you doing? Why would you one: text me all of that? Just cause your baby mama put you out doesn't mean you can just hop back in my life. Two: lying to the kids! They are not for sale or a toy you are just going to play with and forget when you break it!

See, that's where you wrong at London. I do love you and I want my family back!

Family! Back! What! You have to be kidding me. I promise you I'm buying your baby mama a mother's day gift from the heart. She deserves that and you. Anytime you can be a side bitch for damn near an entire relationship says so much. You lucky that I didn't murder that bitch and yal kid when I found out about them.

London! Okay! I don't wanna hear that shit! You was far from an angel ya damn self or did you forget?

Nah I didn't! At least when I did cheat on your ass I made sure to keep you primary, loved, and respected our family enough to not allow any outsider to take your position. That's what you should have did. I know it had to be hard on the side having to get yo ass beat for coming to my house. Watching us celebrate having our daughter. Getting engaged for the second time. Finally getting married and having the dream wedding I wanted. Yeah I guess if I couldn't take you no other way, I would have got pregnant to. Shit what yal getting engaged next? Fuck Out of here nigga! CLICK!

This fool done lost his mind. I can't believe he had the audacity to attempt and try and re-involve his ass in my life, let alone our kids life. How in the hell am I going to fix this shit. Sincere all excited and shit. Ughhhhh! Coffee is what I need. Siyion! I'll be right back! Watch your sister

***************** 2 hours later ******************

Thank you so much girl! I'm so glad you came by and took me and the kids out. I was completely frustrated as hell this morning. I felt myself about to snap, hell I had to go grab some Timmy Hoes! Triple-Triple? You know it! I'm glad mommy called and said bring the kids too. After that shit the father pulled. Honey please! As London puts the key in the door and invites Nye in she barely finishes her sentence. I never been so happy to.......

What's wrong girl You okay? Say something!

Girl you see this shit!

What is it you speak of?

Sir shit! This nigga done brought all of his shit back into my house as if it was okay. Who the hell does that? Shit! He did! What you gone do now? I really don't know. Like what the fuck am I going to do when my mom will be bringing my kids back in an hour or two. He can't be serious, and how did he get in, in the first place is really the question?

He probably kept the key you gave him, or made a spare.

He definitely made a spare! Ughhhhhhhh!

Ding dong! Ding dong! Ding dong!

Who is it?

Toni!

Okay well Nasir not here!

Okay sis! Hahahaha! That's cool. Can I talk to you though? I'm not trying to kick it to you, I'm not that type of nigga. Sir my man and I just don't want to see him fuck up something it's obvious to see is hell'a good for him. Feel me?

(London opens the door) Well I guess so. Like what really made you come here to say that? I can just bet that you helped him bring his shit back in my house as well! Didn't you?

Yeah I did, but at the same damn time I asked that nigga why he was doing this, and what made him take his shit out in the first place You know what his response was?

No!

Neither did he. This is the main reason why I had to come talk to you. I'm going to have another talk with him, but I needed to see what your take and view was on this situation first. Feel me?

Yeah I guess so. Well honestly, I'm not sure what we were doing and are doing at this point. I don't like all the messy shit he comes with. I've explained to him what I've been through and what I don't want to go through again. Like he doesn't seem to understand that.

Okay sis I feel you but there are some things you really don't know about him. I'm not trying to make any excuses for him, I just want you to know this. Nasir loves you. You are all that I hear about.

Yeah he a fuck up. Yeah he do shit that even I want to smack the shit out of his ass for, but he has no one to teach or show him this. He fronts like he knows what to do in life and relationships.

That's a fact! Why is he so damn cold?

Sis that's something you're going to ask him. Honestly he blames his mother and father for his short comings. He really blames his baby mama as she really did my man dirty. Hell he wasn't even locked up 24 hours before she moved another nigga in. Due to that he has never trusted any female he fell in love with. Crazy but he does shit in reverse. He dogs who loves him and loves the ones who treat him like shit!

Toni! I really couldn't thank you enough for taking the time to discuss with me this man's problems. I've not been myself since everything has taken place. My sleep patterns have changed significantly. It seems as though I can barely hold anything I eat down. I've had maybe three seizures in the last week, which have required me to be on light duty! I'm really not myself.

Damn sis! Listen. My man or not, if the shit yal going through got you feeling like this you really need a time out from this nigga. I mean for real. You have two beautiful children that need you. Don't no strong and independent woman like yourself have time for a nigga trying to play games, and confused about what he has and that's real. Believe me! The same shit I speak to you I can say in that nigga face as well.

Well say it to me then (Nasir walks in)!

Nigga you need to get your shit together! Sis really not in no position to be dealing with you and your bullshit yo! She just told me she been sick, throwing up and having seizures.

You need to really get your shit together. You got a good one and don't even know what you have. All the fuck while you was in jail all you did was talk about how you wanted a down ass female, that was good to and for you. You got her and don't even know what to do with her Niggas up top would clown you for real if they knew the shit you was out here doing.

Man get the fuck out of here! Who side you really on? I thought I asked you to talk to London for me, not about me! You starting to make me think you wanna fuck her!

Oh you in your feelings I see, well wake up nigga! Trust me had I had the opportunity she'd be happy, and that's a fact! You won't be happy until a nigga like me, or one you know at that pull yo bitch and wife her! On that note ama leave. Hope you get your shit together my nigga. Bye sis, I'll talk to you later!

Bye sis I'll talk to you later my ass! Fuck outta here with that and she ain't ya sis. From here on out, don't have none of my friends in here without me you heard?

************ Two Months Later ************

Ra'Nae! What you going to do girl? That nigga Sir got a whole girlfriend and they live together. From what the streets saying, that's her car he be driving too! Damn! Like how she didn't know about you? The two of you stayed out riding around.

It doesn't really matter if she know about me or not! I now know about her and that's all I needed to find out. This all makes sense though. Whenever I call him at night his phone goes straight to voicemail. Now all of a sudden it's been a problem for us to see each other. Every time I ask him where he at or what he's doing, he gets mad and wants to argue.

He really been taking the most ridiculous shit and trying to validate it for why he's not talking to me!

Damn that's really messed up. I think I may know where she stays. You know the streets talk. From what I hear ole girl quite, she do a lot of community stuff and she been with him two years.

TWO YEARS! WHAT THE FUCK! WHEN? HOW?

Let me find out some more first. I'm going to take my daughter up to the community center she teach dance at. Maybe I'll get a phone number, meet her, and/or catch him in action.

Bet!

Re'Nae I know that shit had to hurt hearing about it, but you my girl, and I thought you should know!

Yeah it did, but not nearly as hurtful as it's going to be when I smack the shit out of his and her ass too! Believe me when I tell you. I plays the fool for no one. Especially after I majorly looked out putting this nigga on, and letting him use my car to make moves in.

It was now first Sunday and big mama's Birthday. Everyone in Nasir's family loved London and it was only right she attended the service and the dinner. Siyion didn't really like hanging out with the family so he didn't attend, but Sincere she fit right in. Sincere hung with all the kids and always had a great time.

So I hear congratulations are in order for my grandson Nasir and his beautiful and amazing girlfriend London. Before we say grace I want to say may God bless you both with a healthy bundle of joy! This is truly a blessing to hear.

Aww sissy. Muah! I knew it! I knew it! Mama was talking about fish. HMMMMM. Jasintra wrapped her arms around Londn and gave her a huge hug and kiss on her cheek. Awww sis, I knew it was going to happen. Congratulations to you and Sir again!

Ghee thanks Jazz! I hope all is well. We just found out Friday on a humbug. Nasir went out and bought three pregnancy test just so we would be clear. After all three came back positive he woke me up early as hell just to get an official confirmation from the doctor's. He and I both weren't even paying symptoms attention until he started feeling sick randomly.

Damn! How many weeks did the doctor say you were?

Well he scheduled a sonogram for next Wednesday at 2:30 pm so we could confirm his predictions. He feels I may be anywhere from 6 to 12 weeks.

Okay! I'm so excited and I know my brother is too!

Yeah, he's already been lecturing me on what I should and shouldn't be doing. He really wants me to take a break from teaching dance. He feels it's an added stress on me after going to school full-time, completing my internship, being a full-time mom already and doing my daily run arounds.

Yeah sister, I agree! You might want to think about listening to him as well. I mean, you know for as long as I've known you, you have been experiencing complications since giving birth to Sincere.

True, but dance and the kids are my life. Ummm, let us not forget that's how I met you! Hahahahaha!

I guess your right sis, just be careful. I'm giving the baby shower so get ready!

Ha! Guess who's going to be a Daddy!

I don't know brah! Maybe the same nigga who been a father already! Hahahaha!

Toni you got jokes I see!

Brah I knew it wasn't going to be too long. I knew it was only a matter of time. You see I heard London when you moved all your shit back in the house when she said she hadn't been feeling good. Had you been ease dropping correctly you would have heard that shit too, with your soft sensitive teddy bear ass!

Yo stop with all the gay shit! I was never soft, or sensitive my nigga!

Right if you say so! Please don't make me clown you on how all you do is talk about how you love London! How you wish another nigga would try and holla at her! What you would do if she did fuck with another nigga, even though you deserve for her to!

Man shut the fuck up! Like for real doe! Whose team are you on? You stay having London back. You make me think you want her.

Brah I'm only going to tell you this and for the last time. Women like London only come once every blue moon. She's already proven she a rider. You don't have shit and she love you. Like come the fuck on. If anything I'm jealous I didn't see her first

Pop pop pop! (Gun fire sprays through the area Toni and Sir are in)

Yoooooo! Pop pop pop! (Toni returns fire)

Pop pop pop! (Sir hammers back as well)

Both men run to the nearest yard, meanwhile London's truck gets hit in the process of bullets flying through the air!

Awww Shit! They done shot at London truck! What am I going to do now? She's going to kill me! Damn brah looks like you might be moving out again! Hahahahaha.

Noooo! A familiar voice yells out.

Someone call 911!

Help! Help! Sir get some help!

Toni what's wrong? Nooooooo! Oh my God! Not Damone! Come on man get up! Get up man! Get up! Call 911! Somebody help man!

Toni kneels beside Damone and begins to pray.

Lord please forgive me for all my sins. I understand that I may not have honored or cherished your steps, but in this mere moment I ask of your forgiveness. Please let my cousin live to see yet another day. He has always be my strong arm. Without him I may not be able to contain what I will do. Please lord hear my cry as I humbly beg for you to spare this man's life right here.

Yo! They on their way! The paramedics are on their way!

He's dead Toni say's as he closes Damone's eye's. They done fucked up now! Them Up-Top niggas done offed my man and shit about to get real deadly around here. FUCK THE POLICE! I'll handle this shit myself. You with me?

Yeah I'm with you Sir replies.

Go ahead to the house. I'll call you when we squad up!

Toni you sure?

Man go ahead! Do what the fuck I said. Go home make sure London good and just be ready when time comes. I'm good. You need not worry about, but if you will be ready for the work we about to put in!

Oh I'm ready. I got exactly what they need to! Lights out!
(Sir Pulls off before the police show and paramedics arrive)

Chapter Four

" It's Never A Dull Moment!"

Hey my loves! Let's start our lesson plan for today with a light warm up! You guys can pick your music today for this part!

Yayyyyyyyyyyy! (all the girls cheer out preparing for the lesson)

Ms London how about something old school today? We were all thinking since your always so helpful and instructive to us, even when we aren't willing to cooperate let's do something you would enjoy to!

Oh really! Okay! Sounds like a plan. So what did you all come up with?

DJ Easy Roc and Rob Bases song "It Takes Two"!

Now that's a classic. I like! Okay let's get ready!

All of the kids and Ms. London were excited. This was rare that everyone was excited to work-out and participate willingly doing a new routine. London felt a little nauseous and excused herself from the room. While on her way to the bathroom an unfamiliar woman appeared anxious to obtain her attention. Ummmm Hello! Excuse me. Are you the instructor in charge of this program?

Ummmm Yes I am and how may I help you?

Well I was wondering when you would be having try-outs for your team? My daughter is 7 and she really likes to dance. Oh and she's good to.

Oh Okay. Well how did you hear about us? Wait excuse me for a minute. Briyana can you step in and finish warm-ups for me. If I'm not back in time go-ahead and begin competition lesson 6.

The music for that piece is already in the stereo system. My apologies now where were we? Pardon me that's right you were telling me how good your daughter was. Yeah! She's been dancing since she was 3. She used to dance with Sparks on Fire, but has since been wanting to join your team "Devastation" right?

Ring. Ring. Ring.
Ring Ring. Ring.

Hello!

Bae! They was just shooting at me and Toni! Damone got hit and he dead!

What! (London screams loudly and drops her phone)

Yo you gotta get a ride to the house after practice. Calm down okay! Tears begin to stream down London's face. Her voice began to quiver when responding to Nasir saying "Okay".

The news she had just heard was devastating, causing her to shake. She knew she was going to have to repeat what she had just heard but how, is all she could think of. Damone's daughter dances for her, and his girlfriend is a Team mom! All of a sudden a loud scream is heard from the dance room!

Ummmm I see this may be a bad time to get my daughter involved. If I may have your name and number we can continue this at a better time.

Yes I'm sorry! My name is London and I can be reached at 716-253-9667. Thanks. Please excuse me.

Before going to the house, Sir wanted London to see what had happened. He knew stopping by the center with a shot up truck and blood on his shirt was going to scare London, but he had no choice. He wanted to show her just how real things had gotten, while picking up the information for the car. As soon as he pulled up he sent his cousin in to get her. Oh My God! Sir what in the hell happened? Man bae I don't even know. It all just happened so quickly. I was just standing there talking with my niggas, telling them how excited I am to be becoming a father again, and shots rang out all over. I had to react so I grabbed my heat. Next thing you know when shit settled down I heard Toni screaming call 911.

And the blood all over your shirt I guess is Damone's right?

Right!

I honestly don't know what's going on right now but what I can tell you is I'm scared. Like you could have just been killed! It could have been me that received that call during dance saying Sir was killed. When I heard Quita scream after we hung up I knew then she had received the bad news. (London starts crying and shaking again having to have had an instant reflection of the events that just transpired.

You right! Clam down baby please. I know this shit is real, but it wasn't me okay. We're about to have the family I want us to have. Look I know your scared but I'm good. Shit we good and know that! I would never in my life bring harm, put you in harm way or expose you to any kind of harm and that's a fact. You and the kids London.

Yeah baby I believe you. Today has been exhausting enough. I really need to lay down, but I have to go and grab the kids from their fathers house.

Sincere didn't go to dance today?

No. Their father wanted to spend some time so I allowed them both to go with him.

Damn!

What's wrong? What's the problem with that?

Well during the shoot-out, your truck got hit! Sorry!

Sir knew he had to tell her about the truck, and at no time was it going to be easy. Since she needed to use it, now was the best time to tell her!

Sir I can't fucking believe this! My truck has 5 bullet holes on the passenger side with a window blown out. I see you fucking forgot to mention that shit! Like what the fuck! Now London was pissed.

She instantly forgot about today's events as soon as she saw the damage to her truck. How am I supposed to drive around town with bullet holes in my truck. How am I supposed to drop my kids off to school? How am I supposed to go to work?

Calm down bae. For today call one of your home-girls and ask them to take you to pick up the kids. I'll get this taken care of tomorrow I promise. You need some rest.

How do you expect me to rest when Owe! (London experiences a sharp pain run down her side.)

What's wrong? You okay?

Yes I'm fine. Let me tell Briyana that I need to leave and to finish up class. I'll call their father on my way in and ask him to drop the kids off or me. I really need to lay down. I'm sure he will if I tell him I'm not feeling well.

Okay, okay, okay. Well let me help you lay down. I'll lay down with you for a little bit but, I'm going to have to leave when Toni calls me okay? Both get in the truck and hop on the 90 west to go home.

After such an eventful day I would just like to lay in your arms. This way I could give thanks to the Lord for keeping you here and allowing you to protect me from harm.

London. Now is not the time for me to explain what me and Toni have to do. He's good and I'll be too. The less you worry the better I'll be okay. You know I love you right?

Yes I do.

Then just lay here and rest. While your resting say a silent pray for me. Sir kisses London and falls asleep with her while rubbing her back.

Ha! Who's ya best friend ReNae? That's right me!

Okay and?

Well you remember when I told you that I was going to attempt to get shay shay on the dance team of Sir little girlfriend?

Yeah.

Yeah well I managed to get her name and contact information. I don't know what happened but she looked as if something was wrong. While we were discussing Shay her phone rang. Whatever was said on the opposite end devastated her, then all of a sudden a loud scream came from the gym area.

Well that confirms what I just so happened to hear about today.

And what was that? Shit let me know. My nosey ass wanted to stay around and ask, but what happened?

Sir's cousin Damone was shot and killed today, so obviously that was him calling her to tell her what happened. (ReNae balls up a sheet of paper and throws it across the room.)

Okay so how did you find out? What he called you to?

No he didn't call me at all! I found out because Damone was talking to Tracey on the side. See he unlike Sir kept it real.

Tracey knew Damone had a girlfriend and could careless as long as he treated her good and with respect.

Okay well her name is London. She's really nice and from what I can tell about her she doesn't go out or get into much drama. Right before I asked if I could speak with her I was talking outside the gym to one of the mothers. She told me that London is with child and not sure as to how much longer she would be coaching.

WHAT! Did she look pregnant? Are you sure?

Yeah I'm sure and for it being a first time meeting her I wouldn't know. All I can tell you is what I found out about her. Oh and here's her phone number 716-253-9667.

Bam, Bam, Bam!

Yoooooooo! Sir, open up yo!

Bae! Wake up! You hear that?

London, hear what? I'm sleep just like you. Lay back down and get some rest.

Bam, Bam, Bam!
Sir! Yo man come on! We gotta go!

Aww Shit! What time is it London? Damn that's my man Ant! Go get the door please. Shit!

Hello! He'll be right out. You are more than welcome to come in; however, going forward knocking on my door like the police and yelling isn't welcome here.

H-h-h-ello. Um I'm sorry miss. I'm sure my man told you what happened to our cousin yesterday. I'll stay outside, but could you tell Sir that it's an emergency regarding Toni and he needs to hurry up!

Okay! Oh my God! Okay! Sirrrrrrrr! Hurry up, it's an emergency involving Toni! Beginning to panic London slams the door in Ant's face unconsciously.

Damn she sexy as fuck! How the hell he pull that? Ant questions Nasir's abilities aloud walking down the driveway.

Yo what he say London? What he say? Sir yells questioning London while nervously attempting to get dressed. Both panicking, nervous as hell, trying not to think the worse. He just said it was an emergency with Toni that's it!

Fuck! Man, I swear my man better be alright too. Told you had to handle some business, now look Laying up with yo ass done got me off track and my man in some shit. I promise you.

You promise me what nigga? I bet you better not even think for a mere second that laying up with me had anything to do with the business you had to attend to. Hell I fell asleep before you did.

All I know is that my man better be good and that's it! Sir walks out and slams the door behind him yelling YO! Ant what's up?

Damn man. I hate to be the one to tell you this but, Toni done got locked up! Sir shakes his head in disbelief while getting into the car. I told that nigga too call me period! What the fuck! Why he ain't call me!

All I know is that he said you had way more to worry about right now. You announcing you was having a baby and with that fine, I mean with that nice young lady he wanted you to be still. Basically man he was looking out. I mean had you been with him, you may have been with him too.

Right, but that's still fucked up. He was one of few niggas I really broke bread with and gave my last if needed to. That was real nigga shit right there. When's his court date?

That's what we about to go find out now. The fam and team on Brinkman at mama's.

I swear Nasir is Bi-Polar or something. One minute he can be the most loving and amazing man, and then next I want to smack the shit out of him. Hell he starting to make me think I might have a mental health diagnosis or something. One minute I'm happy and the next I'm sad.

Ring. Ring. Ring.

Hello!

Hello may I speak with Miss London?

This is! How may I help you?

Well my name is ReNae and I felt it important that I contact you.

Okay and why is that? Would your daughter happen to be one of our new dancers? If so as per the parental agreement page business hours specifically to address any concerns are Mondays from 5 to 9pm. I am sorry but during my personal time I don't address business matters.

Oh you's a professional bitch I see, well my daughter don't dance for you one, and two I don't have one yet!

What! Excuse me!

Bitch you heard me, and please refrain from giving anyone else that long drawn out ass speech when calling you. The real reason why I'm reaching out to you is as it was presented to me, you fucking with my man!

What! Excuse me! Your man who? And Bitch you right I am professional as hell, but that doesn't mean I won't get hood on that ass either! What's up?

Hahahahaha! Fiesty. I see I hit a nerve. Well back to the topic. What's good with you and Sir mama?

Bitch please you called me, and because you called me it should be more then obvious what's good. Fuck out of here!

Well We've been together for a minute and just so you know he was living here until I put his black ass out. He still calls me and text me. As a matter of fact he just sent me a picture of his dick, telling me how he wants me to sit on it!

Hahahahaha! That's cute. I'm sure, but that's probably all you good for anyways. I'm sure your pussy not far from being out of shape. How many kids do you have? Oh and live with you yeah That might have been so, but bitch that's only because we were on vacation. Not only is he back but we're starting a family, So I suggest you find a new dick to hop on as this one is reserved.

Bitch please! Now you pregnant! I can't believe bitches still pulling that one.

I'm sure, and I guess your broke ass has an Obama phone because had you had a real service, with a real service plan you might have been able to see the pic I sent of your man and I getting the sonogram. So bitch try me when you really got some shit to say other then I'm fucking with your man. Last I checked it's been 2 years and we good over here!

CLICK!

Beep. Text#1 Sir who the fuck is ReNae?
Beep. Text#2 Yeah so you got that bitch London you claimed you wasn't fucking with pregnant huh?
Beep Text#3 I know you read this shit! Who the fuck is she?
Beep Text#4 That's okay when I see that bitch myself you going to regret I found out she pregnant this way!
Beep Text #4 Since you not trying to respond then i already know what it is with ReNae. Fuck you!

Beep Text #5 You ain't shit!
Beep Text #6 You ain't shit and me and the baby hate you!

Yo what's going on man? You deep into your phone and we trying to figure out how we have to finish handling this business. Pay attention my nigga.

Man, my bad. London and ReNae beefing and texting me back and forth so much I can't even respond to either one.

Man yo new baby mama come cold. How in the fuck did you allow ReNae to even claim your ass let alone call yo main bitch? You young niggas really be fucking it up for a nigga like me, I swear.

I didn't have nothing to do with that, I promise you. Yeah I was staying over there but that wasn't shit. At that time me and London wasn't working out so what you thought I was going to do?

Look we got business to attend to right now that's more important than you and your "Jerry Springer" ass relationship drama. Them niggas came in our hood and offed my cousin. A real nigga locked up trying to be a good nigga. He fucked up chancing niggas with no heart! Had he put the right team on we wouldn't be having this meeting right here.

Facts! I was wondering why he ain't call me until you told me. My question for you is where you there? It appears you know more about the situation then the rest of us. I'm just saying, and if the team he had, had no heart what does that say about yourself?

Oh you don't want to go there blood. Ant draws his G26 and Sir reacts drawing his G43!

What you wanna do Sir?

What you wanna do Ant?

Making an attempt to figure out her emotions London was briefly interrupted by a sweet little voice. Mommy!

Yes Sincere?

I'm going to be late to cheerleading. You promised me you were going to make sure I wouldn't be late anymore!

Your absolutely right. Go and grab your bag. Make sure you have everything coach Ayanna put on the sheet for practice too.

I did mommy. I did it all last night, oh and don't forget to give me some money to get my taco in a bag you promised me to

You ready little girl? let's go!

Beep Text#1 London you know I love you and I'm sorry I swear I am
Beep Text #2 ReNae means nothing to me. I know you don't believe me but it's the truth

Ohhh! Now he wants to respond. Well too bad and don't give a care what she means to him. Come on Sincere let's go! Sincere and her mommy pull off

***********Meanwhile************

So that's the bitch right there. She lucky she with her daughter .
The bitch ain't even all that why Sir trying make it out like she the
better choice. The bitch wearing some basic ass all black air force
one's with a "Dots" outfit. Bitch need her hair done too!

True, so what are your plans now Renae? We can't just keep sitting
here, and I know you're not going to follow her and her daughter
around?

Why not?

Why not? Bitch you crazy! I can't believe you right now. Just
know I won't be going to jail with you behind a nigga you wasn't
even with 90 days!

Hater! I swear you a hating ass bitch.

Call it what you want, but I'm just being honest. Had I known you
was going to be on shit like this I would have never gotten that
information for you. That lady has her daughter with her and is
currently with child. How can you be mad at her when Sir is the
one you should be beefing with. It's obvious that he fucking with
her. Sometimes you lose! From the outside looking in you better
off without this dude anyways. Now you can be mad all you want
at me, but it's the truth.

Both of you put down them damn guns! Now! That's the reason
why my son is locked up now. I love all you young men as if you
were all my own. I have never and will not now allow this type of
disrespect in my house. Apologize! Right now!

Sorry Ma!

Sorry Ma!

Accepted and now to each other, and mean it!

My bad

Me too!

Now the police are heavy asking questions about what happened. They have reports from the series of events leading up to all 4 murders Damone being one. I don't know what happened mid-morning, and nor do I care to find out. All's I want is or my baby to be safe. With all the shit going on in the streets today I'm almost happy my son is out of these mean, ugly and misunderstanding streets.

Damn Ma, I'm really sorry yo!

Thank you NaSir! You and Ant have been like brothers to Toni since you were all 5 and 6. I've watched both you boys grow. Remember when you were little I'd make both of you lunches to take to school and give you snack money every Friday.

Sorry Mom!

Ant your mother would piss in her pants if she were still on this earth knowing you just pulled a gun out on NaSir and in my home.

Yes Ma'am I know.

Well court is Monday morning at 9am. I've already spoken to Jeremy regarding how much it's going to cost. You all continue to have your meeting. Just make sure before you all leave you grab a brown paper bag and put your contributions in it. Leave it in the microwave. I don't need to know what comes from who. Just know I'll know who didn't contribute. If you thought any of you were a real gangster, you better ask these streets about mama Shay first!

While the boys were at mama Shay's house London had just pulled up to drop her baby girl off at cheer. Sincere don't forget to give me a kiss and have a great practice okay!

Okay mommy, love you!

Love you more sweetheart. I'm going to teach senior dance today so grand ma will be here to get you. Make sure you bring everything home with you when you leave. I told grandma you could have ice cream after practice and don't try and trick into taking you to "Target" either! You know you will spend all her money up and she'll call me complaining later.

Aww okay mommy. See you later

Whew! I honestly don't know how much longer I am going to be able to do this. I'll be three months soon. Between the constant need to rest. Not keeping anything down and these headaches I don't know (London speaks to herself walking to her car).

Okay bitch I see you, but you don't see me! Hahahahaha! Let's see where your next stop is going to be. Now that you've gotten rid of that ugly ass brat it's time for me to shut shit down.

This is my jam right here. Classic MJB always settles the mood. "Real love....I'm searching for a real love. Someone to set my heart free"

*****************Bam*****************

What the? Who the hell can't drive rear ending me. Ugh, just when my day was getting a little better.

Get out bitch! You was talking real breezy on the phone. Let's see if you really can throw them hands.

Awww hell nah! Enough is enough! Bitch you crazy. Like Sir got some good dick in all but what he put on you must was serious. You playing on my phone and stalking me like I gave you the D!

Fuck all that bitch what's...

Pop! Pop! London hits the girl before finishing her sentence. Starting to get sick of the constant bullshit and having to defend herself is stressful enough. I'm sick of bitches like you always trying to come for me! (Kick, Hit, Punch, Slap!) If Sir your nigga then stalk him. He my nigga and (Punch, punch, bop, punch, punch, bop) I'm not out here looking for your raggedy ass. All of a sudden London feels a sharp pain and lets ReNae go.

Yeah bitch it's on now! You pregnant huh? Well you won't be for long! ReNae grabs London's hair and slams her. London immediately covers her stomach. Just as Renae lifts her foot to stomp London Ant pushes ReNae down.

You see bitch! Smack! This the shit that happens when you the real girlfriend! Spit!

London get in your car. Ill follow you to take it your ca home then we're going straight to the hospital!

Yo! Meet me at your girl house immediately! That crazy bitch ReNae you was fucking with tried London!

WHAT!!!!! Are you fucking serious? Man okay I'm on my way! Oh this bitch done got real slick. She don't even know what's about to happen to her ass. I swear both London and my baby that they both better be straight!

****************** Meanwhile*******************

Bitch get the fuck out of my car! How you just gonna let that bitch try me and jump me with a nigga?

I told you I wasn't going to jail behind you and that nigga. Yeah I told you what happened and who he was fucking with, but never did I think you were going to go insane, stalking her and shit! You stupid! I see why Sir don't want you.

Yeah that's okay though. They got me this time but.

Ring, Ring, Ring!

What!

You know what bitch! Let anything happen to my girl as much as a scratch on her face and ama have my sisters reign on that ass. Should anything happen to my baby now or when it get's here, bitch ama put your ass to sleep. Please believe me! Click!

ReNae begins to cry and places her head on her steering wheel.

Girl was that Sir? I tried to tell you to be more careful. I'm sure he's pissed. Now you done got yourself into more shit then you should have. I gave you information to prepare you, not to do something stupid with it!

Get out, Get out, Get out! I'm done! Over this shit! Fuck him and her!

Come on London! I don't know what's taking this nigga so long but we out! I'm not about to let you sit here when you need to have a doctor look at you. You a pretty tuff little lady I see. No wonder Sir keeps you hidden away.

Hahahaha! Thank you so much! (London starts to blush) I texted him like five times. He really should be here by now.

Well no worries. I'm here that is until he gets here! Damn this girl is fine Ant thinks to himself. Do you have any other children or someone you may need to call while you're going to the hospital?

Yes! I have a son and a daughter. My mother will be picking my daughter up from cheer; however, I need to call my dad for my son He's at Football practice.

Okay cool. I see you a real mom! Hahahaha. You go to school, work and take care of your kids. If you don't mind me asking how did you and Sir even meet?

Okay acting like my daddy, thank you! I'm sorry what did you say?

I asked how did you and Sir meet!

That's a long story. Crazy it was, but somehow it just all felt so right!

Damn! Excuse me but you really are an amazing woman The shit you say alone is #Dope. I wish I were there that night. Maybe.

Maybe what?

Maybe I would have met you first. It's clear Sir has no idea what he has, and trust and believe me you can tell him everything I said to. He's going to lose you if he keeps clowning. I'm just glad I was in the area when this shit went down.

Ouch! Ughhhh! This hurts! (A tear begins to run down London's face)

We here. Let me get a wheel chair for you.

*****************2 hours later*****************

Yo what up, she okay?

She okay? Nigga I called you two hours ago, fuck you mean is she okay? I honestly don't know how you lucked up with this one. You keep fucking up and she gon leave your ass for real. I'm sure Toni didn't avoid calling you for you, he did that for her. She's really too good to be true, and honestly for you.

Dude shut the fuck up with all that sensitive shit. Where my girl at? Is she okay?

Hello Sir! I'm nurse Kathie. If your questioning the status of the patient London she and the baby are doing fine. She said when you arrive to allow you to come back. She may be sleeping but you are more than welcome.

 Ant we good. Thanks for making sure MY GIRL was alright. Sir walks into the back room hence the bass and point he made.

Yeah sure no problem. Better hope I don't push up on her! Ant leaves the hospital giggling, but so serious.

Hey baby you good? Wake up, daddy's here!

Yeah I'm good, but what took you so long to get here? I'm starting to think this whole you, me and baby thing is a bad idea. Since I've been with you it's been nothing but heart aches, pain and drama.

I know and I'm sorry baby. I know you don't believe me but I'm really sorry. I swear this shit won't happen again. I'll change and be the man you need okay?

London! Who is this fool?

Mommy this is Sir I mean Nasir!

Well excuse me Sir but London is my baby! Ever since you stepped into her life it's been chaotic. Even my grandkids can feel it, and she's about to have another one. London baby. You know I'm here for you no matter what, but I think you should rethink becoming a parent again so soon when you just went through so much with Siyion and Sincere's father. This piece of shit doesn't seem to have your best interest in mind at all!

London you better check yo mother and quickly! You don't even know me. Shit I got a mother to ma'am.

Yeah well if she's anything like you than she's a mess to

Mom!

London! Hell if his mother cared enough she'd be here and smack the shit out of him

I do care and that's why I came too! Now excuse me if you will but Nasir is my son right, wrong or indifferent. At this time all of our main concern should be London and the baby!

Ladies! I'm sorry you both have to deal with us being your children and our misfortune's but we are together. Mom it's not him as a person it's the things he chooses to entertain, and mommy number two you know how much I love your son and are aware more than anyone of the type of son you have.

What do you mean by that London?

Sir watch your tone! Yes London baby I am; however, I will not allow your mother to disrespect my child. Now if she wants to discuss this like grown women we can. Hell Nasir will tell you I told him on the way here, how much I love you and wish he would just do right.

Well my sincere apologies ma'am, and by the way my name is Sissily

No problem and my name is Luretha.

Well Luretha maybe we can find some time to discuss the things going on in this relationship. I am not sure if you are aware but this is London's second pregnancy. The first one she loss being jumped by some strange woman he was messing with and then to have been in yet another fight today over him, the same situation could have clearly happened again.

NASIR! Well I'll be damn! No wonder this woman has so much anger in her soul for you. I can see why! I'm so sorry, and can understand should you choose not to carry this pregnancy to term. Finding out what all has transpired has me wanting to tell you to leave his ass alone to. Nasir, I can't believe you. You are your fathers child!

Ma! Ma! Ma! Sir calls out as Ms. Luretha leaves out of the room. See what you and your mother just did! Fuck you! You can kill the baby for all I care! Sir leaves out upset and slams the door while a tear drops out of his left eye.

See I told you London. He's really no good for you. Let's get your things. Your being discharged. Tears begin to roll out of those big pretty brown eyes she has uncontrollably.

Listen, I know your hearts broken London and that's okay. You will heal. Now I'm sure it won't be easy but you will be okay. Remember when you were a little girl. You know all too well what it was like with me and your father.

Right which is why I've fucked up more trying to avoid and do better than what I was exposed to.

Okay miss lady. Well do you want me to come in with you?

No mom I'll be fine. I just want to get some rest it has been an eventful day.

Yes! Well I'll keep the kids for you. Sincere already came and grabbed school clothes for both himself and his sister. Sincere needs her hair done, so I'll have Nye come pick her up and braid it for me.

Oh my God mom you didn't tell her did you?

Suddenly the room was filled with silence.

Mom did you?

Well London.

Ughhhhhh! Thanks mom. Here comes another headache. I'll call you later on! Bye! I can't believe she did that. It's already bad enough I had to hear her mouth. (London walks into her bedroom) Oh so he must have come here before coming to the hospital, why he wants to just throw his clothes all over the floor. When she attempts to pick up a pair of his jeans, something falls out of his pocket that makes her tremble. An infant hospital bracelet that says baby Youngman! It can't be. Nasir's last name is Youngman. Hmmmmm 716-858-4000 Extension 342 please.

Children's Hospital how may I help you?

Tracey Pace please?

Sure one minute.

Hello! Nurse Pace speaking!

Hey girl it's London! I need you to check something out for me. There was a baby Youngman born today. Send me some info from who the mama is to the daddy if you can.

Will do! Call you back as soon as I can!

Ring, Ring, Ring!

Hello!

Hey girl, this is what found out. The baby name is Lansir Youngsmen. He was 6 pounds 11 oz. The mother had him via C-Section, and he was healthy. Now why is it you needed to know all this?

Girl it's a long story. Is his father's name Nasir Youngsman?

Well you know it's still too early for the birth certificate paperwork to be completed, but let me look at the registration sign in log. From what I'm told the father was present so let me see. Yup! That's the name we have registered for the father bracelet.

Oh my God girl.

Are you okay? London? Hey girl can you hear me?

Yeah I'm still here.

I can send you a picture of what the mother looks like and her name if you want. As it appears she works for the same health care system as I. Her room is private and only registered visitors are allowed in.

Okay yeah. Send me her pic when you can. I'm feeling sick an need to lay down.

Okay girl I hear you. You sound like you could use some rest too. Go ahead and lay down. I'll talk to you later. Tell your mother I said hi when you talk to her and kiss the kids for me.

Okay. Will do! Now if this ain't some shit. That bastard! Bet I don't keep this baby. My mom is so right! I don't now and have never needed this type of shit to continue on in my life. I wish I would have met Ant first!

bzzz Text #1 London I love you but you pissed me off and I need a break!

bzzz Text #2 I know you probably don't care and that's cool. I will also understand if you don't want to have the baby.

bzzz Text#3 London I know you see me texting you

bzzzz Text #4 Fuck it. Be mad then. It's all good!

716-891-1897 Mommy! Make my appointment for me, and make it as soon as possible please. Okay baby mommy got you. Get some sleep. I'll text you the information when I'm done tomorrow.

*********** A Week Later *************

Girl I hope this time you really done with Sir. Like damn. It's almost been three years and he still doesn't have it together.

Okay Nye, not now.

Not now my ass. He need to come pick his shit up, talking about he need a break. You know I get up with his man still every once in a while and all he do is pillow talk. Sir does love you but he ain't shit! He so called staying at his mother's now.

I know, as he keeps calling and texting me. I told his mother what I found out and that I wasn't going to keep this baby. She told me she understands and that I made a very wise decision as far as she was concerned. This can't be life for me, I swear it can't.

London I'm sure it's not. You are a very good catch; however, you were just caught by the wrong individual.

Exactly! His mom told me she wasn't going to mention the baby as he hadn't even told her. She said she had heard it was by some random ass girl who was friends with one of his sisters, but none the less she didn't think it was true.

Well do you believe his mother, I mean that is his mother. From what it sounds like to me is he's a mama's boy!

Well I do believe her as she has always been nice and real with me.

That's fine in all just be careful. Just like family can fuck you over, they can be on your side too. Always keep in mind no matter what that he is her son. Her best interest will always be that of his unless he decides to marry you or something. Don't get any ideas either.

Nye shut up! Hahahaha! I think it's time for you to go home.

Yeah me too I'll call you later!

Peace!

So what do we have here? I know you didn't really think you were going to be able to hide my nephew from London, dude really. I seen you calling me. I knew when I saw the 5 missed calls what was going on. When Sunnie called me and said Jazz, Nasir got busted I knew then!

Well why didn't you say shit! Who side are you on anyways? One day your down with your brother and the next it seems as though your against me.

Listen I don't care about anything you're out here doing. You don't take care of me, pay my bills, or provide for my kids. Yes you are my blood brother, same mother and father but you a different breed. You're going to have to get a job if you plan on staying here. Mommy has a fixed income and I help her as much as I can. I'll be damned if you think you're going to "London" mommy and that's a fact. Also this isn't a hotel. Keep all of the bitches you deal with on their street. They are not welcome over here. You know just as well as I know mommy only likes London anyways.

See that's yal problem right there. My life don't revolve around London. I'm a grown ass man. Who do you think you are telling me who I can and cannot have come over for company.

Last I checked I was older and you damn sure wasn't mommy. Well mines that is, so you can chill with all the bullshit.

Yup we sure can chill Mr. Grown ass man. We can chill so hard that when you see that I mean business how cold it's going to be outside on that curb. Brother or not you grown well pay a grown ass bill. Only people living for free around here are the kids.

I swear you make me sick! I love you as my sister, but you really make me sick!

I love you too and good night!

Oh sis, can I use your car. I have to make a run. I'll be right back, I promise!

Nope!

Ughh, I swear I hate you sometimes, and this is one of them!

Aww, and I love you too Good night!

After being at his mom's house now a week Sir was starting to hate it. He knew at this point he had nowhere else to go and boy was he starting to miss London. Man I gotta get the hell out of here. Ain't shit to eat but oodles and nooodles, french fries, fruit cups and chicken fingers all the damn time. It's like 15 kids here all day. My fucking mother not only watching her grandkids but the neighbors kids too! Ughhhhh! She think I'm her little helper and shit too. I didn't sign up or this and that's a fact.

N-A-S-I-R! COME HERE! BRING THE BELT!

Okay mommy. Where you put it? Never-mind I found it. See this the shit I be talking about here.

Thanks baby. These kids now-a-days is a trip. I didn't raise any of you to be disrespectful and I will not tolerate it from any of my kids, kids or the neighbors kids, believe that! SHAY-SHAY SIT YOUR ASS DOWN NOW. ROLL THEM EYES ONE MORE TIME GIRL AND YOU'LL BE PICKING THEM UP OFF THE FLOOR! Nasir grab my purse and go get me a pack of Newport kings please.

Where the keys?

On the table next to the towel holder, and come straight back!

Shhhhiiiiiddddd! This is definitely my opportunity to leave. She has to be insane thinking I was going to sit and help her baby sit.

I wonder what London doing. She really mad as hell at me. She changed her number on me and all that (Sir backs the car out of the driveway). I'm going to take a trip and ride by. Hopefully she's sitting on the porch. I swear I miss that girl. What the fuck be wrong with me.

Ring. Ring. Ring.

Hello!

Hey baby you busy? I need you to bring Lansir some ointment for his bootie. It's really red and I want to catch it before it gets worse.

Yo no disrespect, but I'm far from your baby. Like I'll come bring you what he needs and spend some time, but as for me and you, we were never exclusive.

Hahahaha! Boy you crazy. You weren't saying all that when you kept calling me, nor was you in the delivery room. You brought your whole team here just to see him so don't try and down play me now. I'm sure your little girlfriend mad but who cares. Like I told you the first time we fucked. You were mines and I was going to do whatever I needed to, to get you.

I really don't know what I keep getting myself into. It seems I can't get right for shit. As much as I hate my baby mama for trapping me, I'll still fuck her ugly ass. Maybe I do need some fucking help. London was always telling me I had a problem. Now I' starting to believe her ass. Damn I miss that girl.

I know for a fact if Toni was here he could get me right back in where I need to be. My mom's is definitely going to kill me for keeping her whip, but I have a few things to take care of. Those kids in that house a drive anyone crazy. She needs a "Newport" and I need a bag! Shit to be honest a bag and some good ass head could work to. Maybe I will chill at baby mama's for a minute.

Chapter Five

" Shit Happens"

Girl it's been a minute. I think I do need to get out this house and have a drink. It's been a long 30 days and I deserve it! Nye! Nye! You hear me?

Oh yeah girl. Sorry! I was just trying to figure out which new pair of shoes you don't want, that I could have.

GIRL! Hahahaha, you really a damn fool. I'm about to get in the shower. You think you can be ready in about 20 minutes. If so you can pick any pair you want except my designer knock-off Cristian Louboutins.

Ayeeeeee, okay sissy! I already had my eye on a specific pair any ways. I'll run home, wash my ass, and be back to grab you.

I'll be right here. Ohhh, I'm so excited! I just can't hide it! Yesssss! This shower is everything right now. Ha! I'm looking for a new love baby, a new love, yup! I swear on everything I love, That I'm going to have so much fun tonight. It's been a month without any contact of any kind with Sir. Being able to see the kind of man he presents himself as is annoying. It's almost like raising an extra child. Not sure what his deal is but it's no longer my concerns. When I put on this "BeBe" dress I purchased on sale please believe I'm going to put a hurting on somebody's heart tonight.

Beep, beep!

That's Nye. COMING! London grabs her purse and shoes while running to the car.

Okay girl you cute!

You think?

Hell yeah, and we're going to The Spot! You know all the homies hang out there. I'm sure Sir will be stalking your ass if he's there or soon as he gets word you're out and looking like everything a man would want!

Awww Sissy thanks. I'm glad someone feels that way

Well I'm sure you ain't seen nothing yet!

This is so my song. Let's dance!

" All that ass in those jeans"!

Oh okay London! Yesssss ma! Yesssssss!

While the ladies are enjoying themselves on the dance floor, the fellas all begin to enter in. Each and every one of the crew was fresh. They had a crisp edge, new shoes/kicks, dripping in jewels, while wearing the latest trend in denim. No white tees for this clique. The imprint of the money clip in each pocket was accented by the print only a lady should look at. They were fine as hell and they knew it too. Damn! Is that London? Mommy looking real right. I see why Sir can't stay away. Ant was feeling her already, but tonight he felt she deserved to know. London you looking real good tonight Ma. You making me wanna take you home and show you how a real nigga supposed to treat you. I would never do the shit to you Nasir do and that's a fact.

Ant now is not the time to discuss Nasir. I am out enjoying myself and living life, besides I find it real unattractive trying to dry snitch on the next man.

London, (Ant gets closer with his lips touching the tip of London's ear as he speaks) You and I both know I don't give a fuck about how that nigga feel. I also don't give a fuck if you tell him what I said. That man know what it is.

He real lucky to have you; however, he just too stupid to see a nigga like me is going to be his worst nightmare. Watch!

 Across the room a few of the young-ins still trying to make a name for themselves were holding up the wall peeping the scenery. Is that Sir girl over there freaking with his man Ant?

Word B it is! See that's why we can't trust bitches. Money over bitches "MOB" style all day. That bitch grimey as hell!

Man snap a pic and send it to him. That shit foul. I promise you he's going to hop on the first thing moving to get here.

That's a fact! (message sent) I see why he be dogging these bitches.

135

*********** Meanwhile ************

Yes daddy, yes! Don't stop ughhhhhh.

bzzzzzzz, bzzzzz, bzzzzzzz (Sir picks up his phone)

What you doing daddy? Put down that damn phone and finish hitting this pussy.

WHAT! HELL NAH! BITCH I HAVE TO GO!

Fuck you mean you have to go? What you just gonna leave me and your baby like that!

Man bitch don't even try to pull the baby card. You wasn't worried about the baby when my dick was in your mouth. Fuck out of here. I'm out!

Girl you looking so cold tonight. Hell you even got yo man's man's on you! Yesssssss! That's my sister. I swear I love you.

Thanks Nye! You know I love you too. Let's get something to drink. I'm feeling a grey goose and cranberry.

Yes that sounds good. First round on me.

Excuse me Ms.! May I ask your name, with your fine looking self.

London, and thank you.

No, thank you! My name is Raheem. I work full-time for Coco Cola, I have two beautiful children that I take care of, and I have my own place to stay.

Well damn you just asked for her name. She didn't ask for the story of your life. You so cold sissy niggas giving up background checks for free!

Shut up Nye! Stop being so mean. Sorry that's my sister and she just has an over protective hold on me, for whatever reason, I don't know!

Nah, no problem mommy. Here take my number and hopefully you will give me a call.

Nah she won't be taking ya number brah, as she's a little tied up already! Feel me?

Oh, okay! I apologize. Wasn't trying to be disrespectful. She is beautiful and you are lucky to have her my friend.

Ant! That was not nice, and why you blocking on me anyways.

Man chill London. I wasn't blocking shit! You a new face and niggas like him prowl on females like you.

We as men know who's been hurt and looking for a good time, who's a hoe, and who just really down to earth. That nigga that just tried you, done ran that same game down on every lady in here. He a broke nigga, looking for someone to take care of his raggedy ass. Not to mention he fuck niggas too!

What! Oh my God, thank you!

Right! Now ama slide back over to my table. Just know I got my eyes on you. I promise I'll have ya back. If a good nigga approach you then I'll stay in my lane.

Aww Thanks Ant, that really means so much to me!

Out of know where an all too familiar voice yells out: London! Fuck you doing up in here? London, you hear me talking to you! Fuck you all up in this nigga face for?

Brah, watch who you checking my nigga! Snooze you lose. What now?

What now? Brah who you think you talking to. You know what it is with me, just like you knew this was my girl.

Clown you every bitch nigga. Time London stepped her game up.

Sir steps to Ant, while Ant steps up to Sir. Both men are standing so close their noses could touch. Stop it both of you! Sir me and you are not together first off! Secondly Ant knows that's not how I get down! Both of you need to stop with the bullshit!

Nah London, get the fuck out the way! This nigga was never going to disrespect me and think he getting away with it and that's fact!

What you gonna do Sir?

What you want me to do Ant?

Both men unconsciously pull out. People in the club begin to scream and run. Security not too far away comes over and apprehends both.

Now look at the shit you done did London. I was better off staying in my baby mama pussy!

You right! As you should. Don't worry about me as I'll be in court tomorrow for you Ant!

BITCH!

Damn right and look! (London bends down and pick up Sir's phone from off the ground) Guess I'll be in for a treat tonight, won't I!

You get what you looking for Bitch! Fuck you! While you snooping call my baby mama and tell her and my son to come to court for me. Jealous ass. That's why you mad you can't have kids. My bitch one up on you!

London begins running out of the club crying hysterically! Once again Nasir has managed to hit a nerve. All to pretty to cry but defeated by the mouth of the Devil!

*********** COURT **************

All arise for the Honorable Judge Collinsman.

Look girl is that Sir baby mama and his new baby?

Yup sure is. As a matter of fact I did what he asked and called the bitch! She so fucking ugly. She looks just like him with a wig on! Disgusting!

Well damn! Hahahaha you crazy as hell, but your right too. She do!

She look so mad staring over here at you.

As she should. I can't wait for them to come out. I promise you I'm only here to make sure Ant is okay. I feel bad as he was only looking out for me. It's only right I do the same.

Anthony Markenson! You have been found guilty with reckless endangerment of others, be thankful as no one was hurt. Proof of weapon possession inaccurate as no weapon was found. Charges related dismissed. Possession of narcotics guilty, as 1 pound of marijuana was ceased at arrest. You will hear-by be sentenced to 120 day shot-camp program based on your confession of suffering with an narcotic addiction. Be thankful as it could have been worse.

Mr. Nasir! You too have been found guilty with reckless endangerment of others. No weapons were found as a possessions charge is inaccurate. 1 pound of marijuana and drug paraphernalia were ceased at point of arrest. As you too admitted having a drug addiction you will serve 6 months due to intent to sell and unpaid driving restrictions from a previous warrant.

Sir's public defenders asks to approach the bench with Ant's attorney. Your Honor my client would like it if I could provide important information to his supports. Your Honor (Ant's attorney speaks) we request the same. Okay 5 minutes with and report back to bench! Would the support systems for both Nasir and Anthony please stand up!

Suddenly both London and Nasir's baby mama stand up. Unfortunately both the public defender and attorney proceed to approach London as directed.

What you doing fool!

What you doing!

Gentlemen! This behavior is unwarranted! Be silent or forever hold your peace. You both requested your representation speak to your supports so let that be!

Ma'am! On behalf of Nasir he would like for you to sign off as his girlfriend, representative, and owner of property while incarcerated.

Well Ms. London, my client would like for you to do the same.

London says to Nasir's public defender: shouldn't you be asking her that? (Sir's baby mama stares in the public defenders mouth awaiting his response).

Well no ma'am! He specifically requested to have you sign off on his behalf!

Fuck You Sir! Nasir's baby mama screams out as she storms out of the court room saying: I could have stayed home. You had that bitch call me to come all the way down here for this shit! Fuck you and you won't be seeing your son ever again!

I'll sign for both men thank you gentlemen. They are friends so this small mishap should, I pray repair their bond.

Why thank you Ma'am.

Yes Thank you!

Please tell both I will make a deposit of $100 to each in their accounts when available. This should hold them until they get placed. I'll also put money on the phone so that they can get through.

Well ma'am the first call will be free, just thought you should know.

Okay, and thank you! London grabs her bag and the court papers for both Nasir and Ant.

Oh so you think you all of that huh bitch! You got friends doing a bid over you and choosing you. Fuck out of here. I'm still his baby mama! That's 21 years bitch!

Hahahaha! See that's the problem with bitches like you now. See as a woman I can care less about you being his baby mama because you had that child for relevance. I appreciate your observation because it's obvious who he rather be with and his man. I know your feelings a little hurt especially since you woke up so early to get the baby ready to come down here and get yo feelings hurt. Now had you acted like a lady I would offer you and yo son a ride or maybe even give you some cab fare, but seeing as you mad, continue to wait on that bus. Broke ass!

Bitch you lucky I have my baby with me!

No bitch you lucky you have your baby with you! I'm sure you been known about me as I was never a surprise. You just mad your plan failed.

Yeah well he was just fucking me before that whole altercation happened so what now?

And thank you for confirming that you have wack ass pussy! To see that he got out of your twat to come and see what I was doing should tell you so much! Not only did he get out the pussy but he caught a case due to reckless endangerment. Wait! Not only did he but his man's did too and he hasn't even smelled the pussy. So with that being said take your weak ass pussy, and your weak ass comments and get on that bus. Next time you try to come for me study first!

Whatever! You just mad hun, cause your bomb ass pussy can do everything but give him a baby.

Hahaha! Bet you ain't know I knew that! Seems to me like you need to make an appointment and get yo insides checked out, smart ass!

Tears begin to welp up in London's eyes as that's a real tough topic for her to speak about. London put her head down and walked away!

"Psychological invalidation is one of the most lethal forms of emotional abuse. It kills confidence, creativity and individuality"

(www.Healthyplace.com)

By now I'm sure you understand the dialogue of this book. So many women are effected by a form of abuse daily and don't realize until it's damaged their lives. Pause for a moment and reflect on your own life. Can you count how many cancerous encounters you may have engaged in voluntarily? Did you recognize any forms of abuse? What could you have done different? If your silently being effected/fighting this battle there is help. You are not alone! Visit www.tkaytheauthor.org and fill in the required information needed under the contact page to obtain helpful resources in our area.

Dear London,

I hope that this letter finds you in great health and spirits. Just reaching out to see how you and the kids are, and letting you know I'm okay. Thanks so much for the love before I touched down in Orleans County. As you can see I don't call as I don't wish to be a bother on you. Every time I receive a money order in the mail, it makes me appreciate you even more. You really are something special and I hope you know that. I know from the way shit went down in the club and in court you probably want me to leave you alone, but I can't. In all honesty you are the woman I know God has for me. Every night I pray even though it may not seem like it, but I do. I ask God to work on me so that I can be the man you want and need.

My presentation is difficult as it is hard for me to trust that side of me. Like you I've been hurt too. We as men seem to hurt the ones we love the most and go through hell with the one's we knew from the gate we shouldn't be with. You really have done something to me London and I don't know what it is. I watched you that night at the club, and I watched you in the court room. You stood there like a real woman. You didn't flinch or react to anything that was going on. You stepped up and said you were going to be there regardless for both niggas, now that's dope. I can't say how much I like or approve of it but you have been there for both and I know it.

I wonder is that why you won't visit. Do you have feelings for both of us. I know that sounds silly me asking but I guess it just relieves my conscious. You are really and amazing woman. If I could take all of the hurt and pain away from you I would. Just know and this may sound silly as hell, I love you. I'll write you again soon and completely understand if you don't reply.

Love you girl, I hope you know

Ant

Ma! Ma! Ma! Ma! Mom! Mom! Mom! Mom! Mommy! Mommy! Mommy!

What Siyion? It's Saturday and 6:30 am. What in the hell could you be wanting.

Um mom there was a strange man here. He was walking in our yard. I looked out the window and he was leaving something in the door. You think we should call the police?

WHAT! Oh my God! Okay ummm! Go into your sisters room and stay with her. Take your cell phone and call auntie Nye. I'll go see what's going on. Tell her to get here an quickly.

Okay mom, but what about you. Take your cell phone and call the police. It could be a bomb!

Siyion shut up! Don't scare me just do as I say!

Okay mom!

As London approaches her back hallway she see's an envelope on the floor. She bends down to pick it up reading the print on the front. To my love! When opening the yellow colored envelope folded with a rubber-band around it $2000.00 dollars fell out with a note reading:

I'm sure you received my letter by now. This is just a small token from me to show you how much I appreciate you. I had my nigga who I really trust drop this off for me. Take this money and do as you please. I'm good. You showing me you would and could be there is enough. All I want you to know is that when you fuck with a real nigga. Near or far he gon always make sure he take care of home. Like I said I love you and if it's meant it's meant to be.

Ant

Bam! Bam! Bam! Sissssssss!

Hey I'm right here. let me open the door.

What the fuck is going on? Siyion called me scared as hell. Got me up all worried and shit! Hell I don't even think I put both my tits in my bra! I was trying to get here so damn fast!

Girl it's Ant!

What you mean it's ant? Ain't he in jail until next month, right?

Right, I mean that's what he tells me. Girl come on inside. We're going to need some coffee for this.

What in the hell am I going to do. Ant is so dear and a part of me wants to see what he is about. Nasir has my heart and why I don't know. I've never been the type to mess with close friends, or family like fellas but this is really weighing on my heart. Why is Ant so into me?

Ring. Ring. Ring.

Hello you have received a collect call from: Nasir. The following is an inmate from Orleans County Correctional Facility. Should you proceed to accept this call you will be responsible for all charges accessed. Please be aware all calls will be monitored for security purposes. To accept this call press 2. To decline this call press 3.

Hello?

Hey baby what's up! How have you been? You know a nigga real thankful to have you in his life right now. I swear every time I make an order and shit go through I know it's love. I also appreciate the package you send me last week. A nigga really needed that.

Well hello to you too! I'm very happy you liked everything I sent. Your mom sent the shower shoes, your sisters all chipped in and sent food. As you know I went out and bought the under clothes, polo shirts and sneakers for you.

Damn baby, that's what's up. No lie I was mad as hell seeing that clown ass nigga Ant all on you, and I damn sure didn't think you was really going to call my baby mama. I jive laughed at that shit and said only London. You pissed her off doing that shit too. Of course she blocked my calls and told my mother she's petitioning a last name change and full custody.

Not trying to sound mean or be disrespectful but, care? I don't think so. You did that shit to her. You asked me to call her. The hurt she feels is good for her, as these bitches only feel a small portion of the hurt I feel from you often.

I know right! I'm sorry bae and I promise you on everything when I get home ama make us right. Since I been locked down I've been praying to God for your forgiveness. Matter of fact I called my mom and asked her how much do she love you?

Why on earth would you do that, and what does that have to do with asking God for my forgiveness? I'm just saying!

London I want you in my life permanently. After seeing how another man was flexing over you and one who I used to trust with my life at that made me realize you something kind of special. My mom says she loves everything about you. With that being said I asked her to start ring shopping for me so when I get home I can prove to you and everyone who I really love.

You now have 1 minute remaining!

Damn baby the phone is about to hang up. Just know I love you okay and I'll be touching down real soon. I miss you and the kids. I really miss being up in that pussy to!

Boy Bye!

Your call has been completed!

Did that really just happen? Oh my God! Lord speak to me now! Like what type of test are you putting me through. I have two men who used to be friends trying to win my heart. One is as sweet as I could ask. A real stand up man trying to take care of a home that is not even his from a far. Then you have the other. The real ass whole type who would never miss a good thing till it was gone. Ant will touch down in two weeks leaving Nasir with forty five days remaining behind. Now he all of a sudden has his mother out trying to find me a ring. Crazy part is I'm not even sure I want it. Whew it's hot in here and my breast seem a bit swollen and tender. Let me take this bra off and go lay under the AC.

Bam, Bam Bam!

Just when I figured I'd lay down and get some rest. Now here come's someone knocking at my door!

What's up London? How are you?

Aaaaaaaant! Um, I thought you weren't coming home for two more weeks?

Yeah that was without good time. See my lawyer is the man that's why it pays to have one. Your looking very pretty too if I must say.

Thank you Ant. London's knees begin to tremble as the sight of this man's body is more than amazing. Um would you like to come in?

Hahaha! Nah ma. I just wanted to stop by and see your pretty face, and let you know I was home. These are for you (Ant hands her a dozen of white and yellow tulips). The white one's ask for my forgiveness and the yellow represent the happiness I get from you. Take these inside and make sure to cut the stems before putting them in water.

Awww Thank you Ant. Hahaha! You seem to know a lot about flowers I see. I'm a woman and had no clue what the color meanings were to tulips especially.

Hahaha, that's okay. If it helps any I asked my mom.

Boy you. (Ant moves in and kisses London so passionately she damn near passes out). No! Nnnnnnnno,no,no,no,no! This is not supposed to be happening. Ant I'm sorry but.

No need London. It was something I had to do. Just know this. I am a real nigga, but a man too. I asked God for you and he told me you would be mines. I'll wait, even if it takes a lifetime. I meant it when I said I love you, now see you later. Take care. Oh and thanks again for showing me how much of a real woman you are for me.

Ant enjoyed that kiss. Matter of fact that kiss made him love her even more. All he could do was smile as he walked away trying to hide the erection she gave, and how the thought of her smile made it harder. The entire drive he found himself smiling from ear to ear. Geesh how am I going to get her? I need her in my life. I don't know if I can wait any longer. Straight to the shower it was, an boy did it feel so good.

Ding dong!

Here I come just give me a minute. Ant throws a pair of basketball shorts on and his flip flops.

Ding Dong!

I said. Damn!

Was this a dream or what? How on earth was this happening? Standing in front of me as beautiful as she could be was Sky! Now Sky had her shit with her but she was bad and cold as hell. What's up Sky? What brings you here?

Well I heard a good man was home and I wanted to see if there was anything I could do for him.

Damn girl, I mean no Sky I'm straight. Thanks though!

Okay, well then are you sure. You know I come mean with the cooking and opps (Sky purposely drops a bag with groceries to grab Ant's attention). Clumsy me!

Damn is all Ant could say as he helped to pick up the groceries. Sky was clever and knew exactly what to do to get a nigga attention. Bending over in a summer dress with no bra or panties on exposing just how pretty her waxed pink pussy looked. Well ahhhh, I guess you could come in and cook for a nigga. I mean I haven't eaten a home cooked meal in almost a year.

A year Ant. Hahahaha! You have only been gone 90 if days. Where did that year come from if you don't mind me asking.

Well come inside and I'll gladly explain. You see I haven't been in a real relationship in while. Yeah I've had bitches come through and cook but it's a difference when it's your girl that's cooking for you, you see.

So with that being said are you implying that I'm about to be your girl since you said you hadn't had a good home cooked meal in a year.

No, what I am saying is that yes I'm hungry and sure you can come cook for me. Don't read in to deep and I'm really not looking to entertain anyone but a particular woman right now.

Um! Well then why isn't that particular woman over here doing what needs to be done then? Hell I thought (Ant cuts her off).

You thought like every other female which is yal problem now. Worrying about her will get you nowhere. If she's not doing the things that should be done then the only person who should be concerned is the person who wants it. Stay in your lane. I don't mean any disrespect but did you come here to question me about her or did you want to see what was up with me?

Well I guess you're right. Um can you show me where your bathroom is and take the groceries into the kitchen for me please. Let me get myself together and I'll begin cooking one of your favorite meals.

And how do you know what one of my favorite meals could possibly be?

The street's talk baby. Even I know that!

Yeah well the streets lie to. Who doesn't know that. The bathroom is down the hall and to your left.

Thanks. (Sky walks into the bathroom soon to discover Ant's phone on the sink) Bzzzzzz, Bzzzzzz, Bzzzzzz. Hmmm should I? Yup! To Sky's surprise it's a text from London saying: I'm sorry about today. Please understand that my heart is with Nasir. I love him. Even though that kiss was everything I could ever have wished for, I'm sorry but with him I will stay.

Wow! Right on time. This must be the little bitch he want's. I swear I'm so sick of her always getting the guys I want. Bet I shut this shit down. Delete! and I'll be blocking her text as well.

Yo Sky you alright in there. A nigga getting sleepy.

Oh I'm fine baby and no worries. I'll take care of everything. I promise!

Being locked up was beginning to bother Nasir; however, it wasn't one to let anybody in on his real feelings. What was bothering him and needed to be discussed was Ant being home. Sir was starting to trip remembering all of the slick shit Ant was saying about his girl. He also knew that with all of the shit he had put her through, Ant would be a great catch for her, and would certainly piss him off. These thoughts were so intense, Sir began to write.

Dear London,

What's up baby. I've been doing a lot of thinking and to be honest some shit is really bothering me. I know that nigga Ant is home. While we were both up-top we still didn't speak. Like I need to know have yal fucked? I just can't see how this nigga willing to kill a lifelong friendship over you and he ain't even hit. Feel me?

Now no disrespect as I'm coming to you as a man. My lil homie told me the nigga really feeling you. I swear if I find out anything happened between yal shit is gonna be real for the both of you. Since that man touched down I haven't been able to sleep. All I keep seeing is how that nigga was staring at my lady that night in the club.

Man when I get home we going straight to the court house. Fuck all that story book wedding shit. You mines for life don't ever forget that. Yeah I fuck bitches but on everything I love, it's you who I want. It's you who holds me down and It's you who understands me like no other.

London I love you baby. Please know this. I swear on everything I love that I might murder that nigga I find out he pressing you. I trust you baby an my heart is telling me not to worry, but I know that with all the shit I done put you though my chances of coming home and you being there are slim. My mom even told me she talked to you regarding the ring. She said you sounded as if you weren't really sure about what was about to begin with us or or hesitant for whatever your reasons.

Baby I hope when I get out of this box and am able to call you, I become restored with your love. I had to break a nigga jaw for talking foul about what Ant and you might be up to. He may have been clowning, but I took that shit seriously. Man I can't tell you how much I love you, but I do. Hope to hear from you soon. Matter of fact I wish you come see me. I'll be out in time for visits on Sunday. Think about it please.

Love always

Sir

"Never forget that walking away from something unhealthy is brave even if you stumble a little on your way out the door."

(WWW.Healthyplace.com)

Mommy do I have to go to dance today after cheer? Please can I skip? Granny said she was going to "Wal-Mart" and I want to go to! Please mommy, please?

Sincere yes. You are so freaking spoiled it kills me sometimes. I am however happy that your happy. You and Siyion both have been much, much happier lately. I only hope your father hasn't been filling your heads up with dreams again.

No mommy he hasn't. I hope if I say this I won't get in trouble but, since you and that Sir man haven't been together we have been more happy. I don't like him for you mommy. He doesn't treat you like the queen mommy you are. I pray at night that God send you a man for all of us. I know when I get bigger I'll never date a man like that. He looks like he has cooties any ways. YUCK!

My princess you are, and no you are not in trouble. I'm glad we can have discussions like this. My question for you is, how would you feel if he asked me to marry him?

WHAT! MOMMY PLEASE NO! I swear mommy I'll move in with granny.

Hahahaha! Sincere he's not that bad. When he comes home my plans are to have a family sit down. We can all talk so that way we can all be on the same page. None of us are perfect and there are things about all of us that could use some repairing. Now my baby. All I need you to worry about is landing your triple back hand springs in both forward and reverse order.

Awwww mom! Ughh! Well if you want me to do that and be nice to the man you are going to have to buy me a trampoline then.

Little girl are you bribing me? If so you drive a hard bargain I cannot refuse A trampoline it is.

Yayyyyyyyyy! I'm about to call Siyion. Thanks mommy we love you. Just know we got ya back! (Sincere leans forward and kisses her mom on the cheek while they get in the car)

Coming back to the house after dropping Sincere off it begins to get cloudy. A dark covering starts to form in the sky. Damn! It's starting to look as though it's going to rain bad. Sir is lucky I'll be going to see him tomorrow with yet another package. This time hand delivered. I swear I tell you this man just doesn't know how lucky he is. What's even crazier is that I've hit Ant up just to check on him and he hasn't responded. I guess he's upset with me for choosing to stay with Sir but that's only right. Isn't it? Yeah it is. Well maybe under different circumstances but as for now Sir wins yet again.

Bzzzzzz, Bzzzz, Bzzzzz!

Text Message #1. Sis what's up? I hear Ant messing around with your girl Sky now. Oh boy Robbie told me he seen her coming out the house few times since he been home.

Text Message #2. Mommy grand ma said bring Siyion cleats over before his game Sunday. Love you!

Text Message #3. Mommy Grand pa bought me a new pair of cleats so don't worry about dropping my old ones off. These one's are cool.

Damn this bra is feeling tight! Maybe my boobs are getting bigger. Let me take this bra off real quick. London threw in her passenger seat. I must have been hella important today. My phone is usually dry as hell now all of a sudden 6 missed text messages. London continues to read them.

Text message #4. Hey baby girl. It's mama Lu Nasir's mom. I know your planning on going to see him tomorrow.

Tell him I love him and that I'll send his $50 this week. Thank you so much for being a real woman London. I appreciate you

Text message #5 Damn baby girl I haven't heard from you since I gave you those flowers. Well Like I said I'm waiting for the right time. God willing it will be in this lifetime. Love you girl Ant!

Text message #6. I know you seen me texting you! Let's go out tonight and to The SPOT! They're supposed to be giving Ant a welcome home party tonight! I know you wanna go. Hit me up!

Hmmmmmmm! Welcome home party. That might be nice. What should I wear?

Do I feel like going out tonight? Nope not really. A nigga just came home and everybody wants to show fake love. Who I wish could be there is the only real person other than my brother and that's London. I been thinking like crazy about her. Like do I give up or go all in? Times like this a nigga wish he had someone to talk too. This shit is driving me crazy. I swear to God I've never been infatuated with a woman like this before. Is this karma of some sort? Whatever it is it's killing me!

Bae! Bae! You taking all day in the shower. Hurry up or we gonna be late!

We! We not gonna be nothing! Oh I hope you wasn't planning on strutting in The SPOT with me like we exclusive, now was you?

Huh?

No huh's, you heard exactly what I said. Now you cool as fuck and we been doing real good, but uh if I go anywhere tonight it will be on my own. Sorry baby girl but you not the chosen one!

What! Now you sure do know how to hurt a bitch feelings don't you. Let me grab my shit! I bet if it was London ass over here you wouldn't be talking that shit now would you?

Excuse me? Did you just say.

Yeah you heard exactly what I said. London! Now do you need me to spell her name out for you. Oh that's right you didn't know I knew about that huh? Fuck outta here. She don't even want your ass no way. She still stuck on that bitch ass nigga Sir. You was never winning with that one.

How you know that?

Yeah ya left ya phone in the bathroom when I came over to cook. I saw her text and I read it to before I deleted it and blocked her ass.

So that explains why she hasn't hit me up! Thank God. I knew something wasn't right. My mama God bless her soul always taught me to trust my instinct and gut feelings first.

159

Yeah well that's why she don't like ya ass. You messed up a great thing here and I hope when Sir comes home he beats the fuck out of your ass.

Bitch bye! I see you big mad, and with those types of dreams your bound to be going nowhere fast. Oh and since you talking so much shit. Wasn't you all on Sir dick, trying to steal him away from London, then tried to blame a baby on him when you were already fucking 3 other niggas. Pipe down shorty nobodies trying to wife a twat the whole town done had. Sorry! London wins again and yup she has my heart. Please believe me Sir is already knowing and I'm sure his sleep is bothered. Now get the fuck out with your trash ass and nasty cooking!

Welp there goes my plans to go out! It's raining harder than three gangster bitches, with a mouth full of metal and a cast iron bat. I just got my hair done and I promise you I won't be looking like who done it on my visit tomorrow. Since bae hasn't seen me yet so I plan on making sure when he does, I leave a lasting impression. They say you never miss what you have until it's gone. I guess I better try and text this heffa Nye before she drives over here to get me. I'm sure she will need something out of my closet as always.

Bam, bam, bam!

Guess I wasn't fast enough. Hell I didn't even get the chance to lock my closet! Hahahaha!

Girl here I come, London yells out while on her way to unlock the door. Ummmmmmm! Oh! What the! Ant! Aren't you! Oh! Oh boy!

What London! I can't keep feeling like this. I had been wondering why you weren't calling or texting me only to find out Sky had blocked your number to my phone. I need you and I'm honestly willing to do whatever it takes to have you

Ant I just can't keep allowing you to surprisingly kiss me like that, and after you had the nerve to have had dealings with Sky. I learned the last time how she rolls.

Listen I can explain that! I swear all I did was fuck her, and every time it was with protection. That bitch was purposeful. I needed to get my nuts off and I did. When I came here I didn't dare approach you in that manner did I?

No!

Okay than. That alone should tell you the respect that I have for you. I mean seriously!

Yes Ant I understand but I love Nasir and what is going on isn't right.

So you can look me in my eyes and tell me you haven't thought about me?

No!

So you can look me in my eyes (Ant runs his hands down London's waist) and tell me you haven't imagined making love to me?

Uhhhh!

Have you?

Uhhhhh!

Have you London?

Yes! Ant Yes! Are you happy now knowing that I feel you possibly could be everything I've ever wanted and more.

Then let's see London. What happens tonight stays here. I'll walk away after knowing I've tried everything I could and allow you to be happy with him, but first I must. Ant kisses London so deep that her knees instantly go weak. As London enjoys Ant's kiss he picks her up from the floor and carries her to her room. Laying her down on top of the bed he carefully spreads her legs. Gnawing intimately at her pussy while not removing her panties. No she moans; however, meaning yes. Her juices begin to flow ever so deep she allows him to remove them. Soaking wet by now they were.

London Ant calls out asking may I please make love to you? Yes she replies with a soft voice, and gentle touch. She caresses the top of his head as he orally pleases her. She thought to herself how amazing it was.

Ant was slow and fast. He sucked places she never knew could be sucked. He licked and kissed her where only she enjoyed when playing with herself. Oh my God Ant she softly screams out! He lifts his head just before she nuts and says I'm not done with you yet.

Kissing her body from her feet to her forehead London. Yes Ant? are you ready? For Uhhhhhhhhhh London begins to moan as Ant goes inside of her. That moment was everything they both expected, but sadly didn't last long. Oh my fucking God! Damn! Noooooooo! Oh my what's wrong? This shit is too good to be walking around the town without a ring on it! The fuck! I swear I'll make it up to you. No need as it indeed was magical!

Now I could and want to lay here with you all night, but you know they are giving me a welcome home party tonight! I just couldn't attend without seeing you first.

Well I was going to come believe it or not. Hell I was on my way. Speaking of on my way, I wonder what happened to Nye? I actually thought you were her! I swear somethings funny as she would have blown my phone to pieces.

Hahahaha! Well I guess I can say I had something to do with that! Nye cool peoples and from the looks of it, she would rather you be with me too.

Oh so yal just gone jump me now huh? Well it worked. Ant I seriously don't know what to do. As much as it felt so wrong it felt right. Like I don't really know what to do. How in the hell am I going to see him tomorrow. Ouch!

What's wrong?

I don't know but my breast have been really sore lately especially the one your laying on now.

Want me to kiss it for you?

Okay now! Shouldn't you be getting ready for your party.

Yeah. If you don't mind can I shower here. I'll just put back on what I had on. My fresh is fly and you know that I am that type of guy.

Yes I do! Here's a dry towel and the wash cloths are in the drawer closet to the window.

I wish you were coming, but I truly understand. Tell that nigga I send my love and pray that you tell him your leaving him.

You a mess. I'm going to get ready for bed and I'll see you soon.

Feeling like the man, but incomplete, Ant walks into the night club "The Spot". Damn my nigga what took you so long to slide through. We almost thought you wasn't coming. The strippers been here for like 2 hours waiting and shit! 5 bitches brought you cakes and shit like it was your birthday or something. Man what it do! Niggas really happy to see you. Let's go.

Okay! Okay! Alright now! Ya man is home. I was on time out due to some fuck shit, but you know a nigga back. Let's get lit!

That's what I'm talking about. My nigga. Yo you seen yo brother Mikey. He want you in the back by the bar. Meanwhile ama go get the bitches and we gone set this shit off right! Yo I need a bottle of 1738, ACE, Grey Goose and Moet!

Hi Ant! You looking nice tonight. You coming home with me?

Hi Ant! What's popping baby. I missed you! Glad you home. Maybe we can pick up where we left off

Hey baby, you missed me? I missed you. I know you been waiting on a good woman and I'm sure I can fill that void.

Now this the shit I don't miss. Damn I miss London ass. I wish she would just.

Hi Ant surprise! I hadn't let you down yet so I figured I'd slide through and come pay my respects. Welcome home.

Ant! That bitch was never invited yet allowed back in here after the fuck shit she caused between you and my nigga Sir. She the bitch that got you both locked up on some fagazey type shit, you know what I mean?

Nah I don't know what you mean and ama ask you once and once only to apologize to this young woman and shut the fuck up. Ya boy a clown and been a clown. He was the one all in his feelings. Shit she cold and if he knew better he would do what he need to by her. So before you talk some ole grapevine type shit speak your facts. She held both of us down while locked up.

Awww damn my apologies ma. Would you like something to drink?

No and your apologies accepted No harm done as I understand. If it is uncomfortable for you and your friends to see me here I can leave.

Hell no you won't. Just sit tight love and anything you want is on me. You and your girls. BARTENDER! Whatever these ladies right here want it all on me.

Okay got you and welcome home man we missed you here!

Hahahaha! They all act as if I was gone and did a real bid, but I guess when you show the town love they miss it when it's gone.

Look the party is about to turn up a bit and I don't want you out to late. Have some fun. Drink a drink or two and then I'll see you later!

Later?

You heard me. I'll see you later. Bye for now my love!

Damn girl that nigga sure is sprung!

Shut up Nye and order your drink! The ladies all chuckle together an begin placing their orders. After three good rounds the ladies decide to leave and take it in. Nye was so tipsy she wasn't paying attention to the cab following behind her car. When London gets out she is nicely greeted

Now you know you shouldn't be here. It's 4 am and I'm going to see Sir in the morning.

London, need I answer you? I'm starting to think you like hearing yourself talk or your trying to convince yourself that how you feel about me isn't real. Sorry ma it is and I'm right here Live and in person. I couldn't wait to leave that party. I took a cab over just because people be watching. All out of respect for you baby. Now come over here. You know you want too.

I do, and maybe you are right. I don't know why wrong shit feels so right, until it hits the light.

Well I told you already I've discussed this with God. On my life I know what's right and I promise you, you will be fine.

I hope so Ant I really do.

They both stare into one another's eyes preparing to pick up right where they left off earlier.

London began comparing them both sexually to herself as Ant thrust deep inside of her. Ant began feeling as though he was winning and planning what exactly he was going to do when Sir touched down. The way they made love, and fucked. Made love again and fucked. made love again and fucked you would have thought they were destined to be. They both lay down passed out, sound asleep until.

Ring, ring, ring!

Hello London says sounding as sleep as she was.

You have just received a collect call from: Nasir! The following call is from Orleans County Correctional Facility. You will be responsible for all charges should you chose to accept this call. For quality assurance this call maybe monitored and recorded. Press the #2 to accept and #3 to decline.

Yo what's up with you? Why the fuck you sounding all sleepy and shit. I see you ain't wanna come see a nigga too.

IIIIIII wasn't feeling to good baby, I'm sorry!

Sorry! Fuck you think am stupid or something. I know you was at that nigga Ant welcome home party last night too. Yeah I'm starting to think you and that nigga got some shit going on. I can feel it. London looks down at Ant as he lay sleep on her thighs.

Yes I was there and so what I'm grown. I had every intention in the world on coming to see you but when I awoke I wasn't feeling well. My chest have been hurting like crazy and I was throwing up.

Instantly Sir starts to think London maybe pregnant and quickly switches his tone. Hoping that she is as that would only make what he was so-called planning go so right. Sorry baby you know I just miss you.

Yeah but you can't keep treating me like these bitches you deal with regularly. Oh and how I know when you do come home you're going change and be a man of your word.

Ant hears that and starts to smile. Suddenly he begins to lick on London's clit while she talks to Sir on the phone.

I swear baby I am. I promise you I know you may not believe me but for real I am!

Yyyyyyeah I've heard it all before. Matter of fact you pissed me
off! Click! Ohhhhh shit! Ant you really trying to get me in trouble.

I bet it felt good to hang up on that nigga?

It did but nowhere near as good as how I feel right now.

Good Ant replies and prepares to place his dick inside of London's
wet pussy. He was oh so ready and while he stroked her, she dug
into his back. He said a silent prayer as the love he felt for her ran
ever so deep. This was now turning into something so deep even
Ant wasn't sure if he was ready for what was in store.

Since the last time they made love Ant couldn't seem to stay away
from London. They both seemed to enjoy each other so much, I
believe they forget about the situation at hand. Ant! Stop playing
with me. You know I hate when I'm cooking and you stand behind
me trying to help me cook rubbing on my booty!

Well what you want me to do. I mean you are in my house. Damn
near naked, and you want me to just sit down like a good little boy.
Fuck out of here! You fine as hell. Smart as shit. An amazing
mother to your kids, and can cook your ass off. Child please if you
ever thought I was just going to sit here you had to be nuts! Ant
giggles and kisses London on her cheek.

Ant what are we doing? Seriously. You and I both know Nasir will
be home soon. We know that I haven't actually gotten over him
yet, but are aware that I have feelings for you.

You just made a great day turn blue. I haven't been thinking about
you and that clown since my coming home party. We have been

fine for the last month and now you want to talk about it. I say just let nature take its course. Either way I support you. I love you and I want you, but as I told you in the beginning I understand.

Awww duka! Yeah right!

Don't call me that! Hahahaha!

What you mad Mickey told me your nickname.

As a matter of fact I am. Why would he ever. I told him when we were kids the only woman that could call me that after our mother passed away would be my wife. Now if that's the title you want you can surly have it, hands down.

Yeah right! I know one things for sure and that's I want to be proposed to romantically and have it be so special that I will always remember it no matter what!

Well first off you have to allow a real man to do it. You keep chasing after these clown ass mother fuckas you gone get what they give. Take it or leave it.

Your so right! Damn I never thought of it like that.

Well Like I said keep fucking with clowns and you're going to be co-starring in their comedy. Now come here. You know what time it is. I honestly hope I get you prego before that man comes home. Lord knows I been trying.

Hahahaha! Oh so niggas trap females too I see. Nope that's not going to happen as I don't get prego that easy. London thinks to self maybe I need to make sure that I'm not as ever since Sir left my chest has been hurting and my clothes have gotten a little bit tighter. No I can't be! Can I?

Chapter Six

" The Signs are all There"

Hey mommy!

Hey baby girl! I see you went and picked up my big baby boy! Give mama some suga!

Ma! Stop! I'm grown!

You still such a big baby, but I love you. Hand me my pocket-book. You know I have something for you. (Sir's mom hands him his phone, wallet, and the money he had in property)

Ma! How you get my belongings?

Well Sir, London didn't want the stress of it with or on her. The temptation of the devil was present. We prayed together when temptations were massive so she asked me could she bring your belongings to me.

Wow baby! Forreal?

Hell yeah! Opps, I meant yes Sir for real. I'm sure that had I looked in your phone I would not be standing here with you today.

Your so right! I never. Well I forgot to think about that! Man ma let me talk to you for a minute. (Both walk into her bedroom) Ma did you find a ring for me?

Sir in just being honest London deserves a ring worth more than $100 dollars. I didn't want to hurt your feelings when you asked so I just waited for you to come home. When you love someone and recognize the blessing God giveth you. You do more than the bare minimum when you can. To me you are being cheap and selfish.

This girl has been the best one you have ever had. Lord I feel the spirits talking through me! Amen!

Aww here you go now with your church bullshit! How are you going to tell me how to spend my money and what I should do with it!

Son, I speak the Lords truth only. What h see fit I say, I deliver!

Well where was the lord when you was on that crack pipe leaving us to take care of ourselves? Where was all the spirits when we had no food and was out here stealing from the stores just to eat? Where were they when we had no lights and gas sleeping in one room all bunched up so we didn't get sick? I had to wash my ass at school a many of days. Stealing socks and bullying others because I didn't have shit! Yeah now let's not forget about those days. I tell you what. Since you did. How about I leave them demons right here for you to talk with! I'm gone! London let's go! I need to make a couple of stops anyhow. Ride me down the way first.

After they both get in the car Sir pops in his "Jada Kiss" CD. While riding and happy as hell to be home he spots a couple of his peeps. Yo! What up nigga. Pull over girl. I'll be a quick minute. Sir hops out and all his niggas are happy to see him. It's about time nigga! Glad to see you home man! Shits been crazy out here with you missing!

Hell yeah! I'm glad to be home too! Shit I missed seeing these streets, my niggas, family and my wifey.

Okay, okay, okay! Good seeing you. I know what it's like first day home in all just seeing wifey! Hahahaha!

Right! If she know like I know I'm about to tear that pussy up! Grrrrrr!

Boy stop acting so crazy, and why you putting people all in our business.

Oh what you don't want nobody to know our business all of a sudden with yo thick ass. Damn like you got sexy thick while a nigga was sitting. Hey! Excuse me Mrs? You see this woman right here? I'm about to marry her!

Oh congratulations young man. I'm so happy for you. That's exactly what young people should do now a days.

Yuppers! That's just what I'm going to do.

Hahahaha! (London was tickled and started to blush) Nasir you crazy. Come on and let's get home, I'm tired.

Tired? It's Friday! How the fuck are you tired on a Friday?

I do work you know!

Okay! You right. Can I just stick the tip of it in you real quick though? That skirt is driving a nigga crazy. You know I haven't been up in that pussy in Lord! I don't even wanna think about it!

Shit! My dick is hard as fuck! London! Oh my God! Please help daddy, please!

Maybe when we get to my house you can put the tip in real quick but nothing serious until we get home. Ouch!

What's wrong baby?

I don't know. My stomach just started cramping out of nowhere.

Nah, nah, nah! Don't try and play me with that shit! Who you been fucking cause I know mother nature not about to surprisingly pop the fuck up!

Hahahahaha! No stupid, and to be honest me and Mother Nature need to talk. I've only had one period since you left!

Okay! Sounds like some shit I wanna here! When do we need to go to the doctor's cause as you know I'm going to be right there! Shit, this is what we both been waiting for and needed.

I'm not so sure about all that but I will be going and soon as I know something isn't right. Here we are. Home at last!

Before they could get out of the car Nasir's phone rings; however, from the ring tone it was only his mother. London went on in the house as it was none of her concern what they were discussing anyways. London thought that would be good timing for her as she wanted to text Ant anyways.

Boom! The door shut so hard the pictures on the walls began to rock. What happened?

Man don't worry about that shit! What happened, happened, and it happened for a reason. Sometimes I don't know who my mother fucking think she is but I am grown as hell now, and that shit from when I was a kid really pisses me off. (London notices a tear roll down Nasir's face)

Well I'm sure everything is going to be alright in time.

Man hand me the keys. I need to go pick me up some smoke and grab us something to eat. Let me ask you a question though and be real honest with me! If all I had was a hundred dollars to buy you a ring would you wear it?

Sir, price isn't a factor with me, meaning, effort and intention are!

Fuck you mean by that?

That if you were struggling and I knew the love we had was real, authentic and exclusive I wouldn't have a problem. Reason being is because if my man is struggling I must be too. When to people are together everything is done as a collective unit.

What the fuck did I ask Ms. Social Work for! Geesh! Okay, never-mind and thanks.

Well you asked and whatever issues you and your mother have need me taken care of with her. Lashing out on me will get you know fucking where. Shit! You don't even know what you have no how. It's plenty of men wanting to be the man I want anyways.

Bitch what! Pop!

Nasir did you just slap me! Oh my God. Get out! Get the fuck out of my house right fucking now!

I'm not getting out no fucking where. You got a real fly ass mouth and I'm starting to think you been fucking another nigga. You have never spoken to me like that before. we'll see.

What do you mean by that?

Bitch you'll see!

London sits in the bathroom secretly crying. Asking God if this was her punishment for cheating with his friend. Suddenly as Nasir stands on the porch, Ant pulls up.

What up!

What up!

Both men speak but keep it cool. Ant peeps somethings wrong with London and starts to get upset. He wants to flex but can't. Instead he handles business and drops off the work for Nasir, but it appears Sir is up to no good trying to be spiteful.

Yo let me get a pound of that good shit! I'm about to roll up, eat and fuck the shit out of my bitch! Sir speaks loudly just so Ant can hear him and he does. Making an adverse attempt to leave before facial expressions give him away Ant creates away to hurry Nasir

out of his face. Thanks for the paper my nigga. Me and my bro
Robbie about to get this neighborhood block party cook-out
started.

That's right, that's right! I'm sure all the homies gonna be there.
Maybe you can bring the kids and yo girl out! It's a big block party
today ya boy Ant and my brother Robbie for all the fallen soldiers
kids. We brought bikes, sneakers, outfits all kinds of shit for the
kids. You know we do! We're big on shit like that but you knew.
Real niggas.

I don't know! Hahahaha! I just might bring my soon to be wife. I
planned on taking her ring shopping today as a matter of fact. You
know what? Hell yeah we will be there kids and all.

Bzzzz, bzzzz,bzzzz.

Text message #1. Shorty what's wrong you okay? You know all
you have to do is say the word.

Reply from London: Yes I'm okay. I just think what I did was
wrong and now in some weird way I'm paying for it!

Text message #2. You looked so happy when we were together.
Bae you had a glow. Now all I see is hurt and pain. I want so badly
to come and rescue you.

Reply from London: I don't know Ant. You and both know that Sir
is home now and I have to do what is right. I hate saying this but
please don't contact me again

Text message #3. If you say so shorty! Just know that I love you and I tried to expose you to a real nigga. Your choice!

Ughhhhhhh! What the fuck am I doing! (London put's her head down and begins to cry harder) Why lord is Nasir so fucking evil. I can't believe how he hasn't even been home 24 hours and already he has managed to hurt me. maybe everyone is right! Why am I putting myself through this shit!

Bae I'm sorry. Let's fuck so I can bust this nut then I have a surprise for you!

Sir attempts to eat London's Pussy. All while he sucked and nibbled fast and sloppy London thought of how good Ant pleased her. Ant made love while pleasing her orally. Sir was eating on her as if this was his first meal and the nigga was suffering from starvation.

You ready for this dick? I know you is! Ummmmmm yes this pussy just as wet and tight as I left it! (London says to herself no nigga that's vinegar and water with a proper tighten from a real nigga beatin it up) Ohhhhh. Yesssss. Okay daddy London says just to stroke Sir's ego.

DAMNNNNNNNNNN!

I'M!

CUMMMMMMINGGGGGGGGGG!

Oh shit girl your pussy is good. Go cook me something to eat. You want this ring don't you and we going to the cook-out!

The cook-out?

Yeah! Why you say it like that? A nigga fresh home and I'm claiming all of what's mines. Why you don't want to go?

London know's this is a trick question so she answers it perfectly. Hell yeah I wanna go! It's time to let these bitches see just who the queen is!

As sure as my name is Sir, Yes Ma'am your right. Now girl hurry up and cook a nigga hungry as hell.

Once they took a shower and was fully dressed London started to think that going might be a bad idea. She didn't know how she would feel if Ant saw her kiss Sir or hug him or what. She was very nervous and started hesitating just a little. Unfortunately Nasir was ready so it was time to go.

Hey! I would like to take the time out and thank the entire community for supporting me and my brother Ant's community event!

We love you Ant! A female shouts out of the crowd.

Hahaha! And I love you to Ladies.

We have done this same thing every year since we lost our bigger brother. As most of the town may know, we lost our parents at a very young age. Our brother was all we had to mold us. To honor someone so special in our lives we have decided to do this event in his honor. Just as he never let us go without. We do our best to make sure our communities children have. So eat up and enjoy your day.

Ah Ha! Yes Sir! Ya nigga home fam, ya nigga home!

Okay, okay, okay! I see you and the misses looking real fly!

(London try's to smile) You know a nigga had to come home and get fly. You see me and my soon to be wifey. Bae showem the ring!

(London hesitates, but covers) Aww bae you too much! I wouldn't want the hate in the town to block our shine already.

Okay, okay, okay! You heard the wifey. Yeah this how a nigga supposed to come home. Get fly, stay paid and make sure he take care of his own.

Okay I see you Sir! Well congratulations on the proposal and I wish you both the best.

Ohhhhhh girl did you hear that? Sir done proposed to the bitch London. Ohh we! Wait until Sheeka hear about that.

Shit Sheeka! His baby mama!

Ain't that her over there?

Yes girl yes! I'm glad you made me come out today! Shit's about to go down.

After hearing the news Ant walks by with a cutie holding his hand. Congratulations on the nuptials and let's squash this beef. Looks like you happy and that's all that matters. London is an amazing women and you need her. Take care of her and you two enjoy ya time here. London starts to turn red. Trying to hide the fact that she is pissed seeing some random chick alongside Ant smiling was making her sick. Instantly she throws up. Oh my God I'm so sorry, so sorry, so sorry!

Ant now concerned turns around and looks worried. He begins to think damn is my baby pregnant? The little cutie he was with releases his hand and starts to walk away. Sir's baby mama notices the crowd gathering around London and with Sir right by her side.

Sir! Sir! Sir! What you forgot to tell your family you was coming home I see. Yal looking all nice and shit. What about yo baby huh? I see you didn't make time to have him match your fly. Oh and not to mention where's my fucking money you so-called needed to get back on when you touched down? I know this bitch ain't wearing it!

Yo chill bitch and get the fuck out of here talking that jealous shit! You just mad I didn't put a ring on yo finger.

What! A Ring! You gave that bitch a ring when you promised me you was going to get me one when you came home!

London looks up at Sir and busts out in tears. She instantly runs away to hide from all of the embarrassment, while thinking how this would be a good time to tell Nasir no good ass she wanted to be with Ant.

Damn brah! You keep all the bitches mad! A random homie walks up to say. I swear you a genius. The bitches be mad and still fuck with you! Pimp shit! you the truth.

Man cut the shit! I ain't trying to hear that right now.

London, London, London! You okay shorty? What's wrong?

Ant I can't! Please just leave me alone. It's already enough shit going on right now, and I don't need you making it worse.

Baby girl you know.

What that you're never going to hurt me! You got me! Fuck out of here with that shit! I saw you and little shorty all hugged up! Your just like Nasir! No wonder your friends.

Associates!

Whatever! Leave me alone Ant please!

Hey Sir how you doing daddy? I see you have a lot of messy shit going on right now but when you ready for a real lady let me know. My number still the same. I would love to suck you down too, with yo sexy ass. The ladies all fell for the man Nasir displayed himself to be.

Alright ma I got you.

Hey Sir! Come here. I see you looking real good coming home in all, but I have a question for you.

What up?

Why you trying to wife her? I know she pretty in and all but rumor has it she was fucking with ya man Ant while you were locked up!

WHAT! How you know? Who the fuck told you some shit like that ma huh! (Sir starts to swell up and sweat while grilling the young lady so hard she dropped her soda and started to shake).

Ummmm, Well I just heard it and was asking!

Asking yeah okay bitch! What you wanna see some shit don't you. Get the fuck out of my face. You ain't shit! Bitches always up to no good. You just mad ain't nobody wife yo retarded ass.

As Sir begins to walk back to the car he notices Ant sitting with his head down close to where London was in her car crying.

So you was fucking my bitch while I was up-top huh! (Ant hops up quick)

Yo you really don't want it my nigga. I done already spared yo life twice. They say three times a charm

Fuck you nigga what! (Sir pulls out his hammer on Ant. As London attempts to get out the car Sir pushes her back in aggressively)

Listen that's yo girl and instead of taking the time to enjoy something so beautiful as a union you letting the streets take away what should be the most important thing in your life right now. Like nigga smarten up. You lucky as hell and don't even know it.

Get the fuck out of here and take care of your shorty! (Ant tears up as he looks at London crying and wanting so badly to rescue her)

Yeah you right. Damn you right. As much as I've put her though I slipped up for a second and almost let a bitch get me. London doesn't need to stress either as she might even be pregnant.

Pregnant! (Ant says sounding surprised, worried, and happy at the same time)

Yeah she has an appointment this Thursday.

Well congrats early. Take care of home. That should be any man's number one priority and leave all this sucka shit alone!

One!

Two!

London, I'm sorry! Like I really be putting you through so much. I know I don't deserve you, but can we talk this out.

Talk! Hell no! Here, and I don't want this cheap ass shit ether! I should have known you wasn't shit! Give it to yo baby mama as she likes left overs anyways.

London please!

Sir please leave me the fuck alone. I'm sure you have other bitches to attend too.

London I only want to attend to you. Ant was right.

Ant? What does he have to do with this Sir? Wasn't you just accusing me of having something going on with him when you were in jail, while all along you were so called blocked from your baby mama. Let me guess that was before or after you told her you were getting her a ring too? Fuck you Nasir and I mean it!

London you know you love me. Please take my ring back. I promise you as soon as I get my money up I'll buy you a new one.

A new one! Why? Just take this shit back to the store and that way you can give ya baby mama her money back she fronted you!

Damn girl I know I fucked up but I'm sorry. I need you and I want you. I'm willing to do whatever it takes to get you back and I mean that. Please put this ring back on your finger before we go inside.

We go inside! Inside where? Here? Hell no you won't be coming in here. Thanks for the ride, but I'm done! (London gets out of her car grabs the keys and goes inside).

Ughhhhhh! Why? Why did I allow myself to go through this. They say the strong survive and God only send his strongest warriors into war, but why me? Why me lord. I'm sick of this shit! Nasir can kiss my ass. My kids were right, hell everyone including Ant was right! This nigga don't even respect his mama, so how could I ever think or believe he would change for me. (London falls onto her bed and continues to cry)

Bzzzz, Bzzz, Bzzzz Text message #1. London I'm so sorry baby please talk to me

Text message #2. I know you don't want to hear from me shorty but are you okay?

Text message #2 reply: Yes I'm okay well now that you texted me I am. Ant I can't lie but I miss you!

Text message #3. Baby please talk to me. Can I just come over and lay down with you. I promise I won't touch you. Please.

Text message #4. London baby you have to choose. If you tell me you want me we good. I can move you and the kids to another location in 10 mins. just say it!

Text message #5. I also overheard Sir saying there is a possibility you could be pregnant. is that so? If so how far do you think?

Text message #4 reply: I know Ant but how is that going to look. I mean I love Sir and I can't deny that, but crazy as it is I think I love you too.

Text message #6. Okay London damn. I love you baby. Please just give me one more chance. I promise I'll go to counseling in all that if you want me to.

Text message # 5 reply: I honestly don't know anything and am just as curious as you are to know myself.

Text Message #6 Reply: Leave me the fuck alone Nasir. Go text one of your other bitches. We done!

Text message #7. I know this may be wishful thinking but I hope you are and that it's mines. I mean would you keep it if it was?

Text message #7 reply: Oh my Ant. As though as it would be to answer that I would say yes. My only reason being is that I wouldn't want to mess my body up of have God punish me anymore.

Text Message # 8. I love you London, I really do.

Text Message #9. I love you shorty I swear, I do.

Text message #8 reply: Awww Ant I love you too!

Text message #10. BITCH YOU DONE FUCKED UP NOW!

Oh my God! Look what I've done. What the fuck am I going to do? I know he's going to come here and act a fool! What in the hell am I.

BAM! Down comes London's door as Sir kicks it in.

Okay Bitch! So you and that nigga Ant tried to play me today huh!

No! No! No! Sir it wasn't like that! I just said that to make you made! Hahahaha! I was joking. Please!

SLAP!

Oh you was joking huh! Give me yo phone than. Let's see just how much you were joking then.

No Nasir I'm not giving you my phone and stop. Sir grabs London by her neck and begins to choke her.

London fights as much as she can until she drops her phone on the floor.

Ohhhhh! Okay so this nigga was texting you the entire time you was texting me. Now talk about me being slick! Bitch you got me beat! Pow! Sir strikes London in her face causing her lip to bust open. Slap! Sir follows up with a swift hand to her right cheek. This nigga want you to have his baby huh? So you know what that tells me don't you? (he kicks her) Don't you? Yup that's right! Yal been fucking.

Ring, ring, ring!

Hey shorty you okay?

Hell nah shorty ain't okay mutha fucka! I gave you a chance earlier today but please believe now that I know what went down nigga that's yo ass on site!

Nigga where is London?

Awwww you sound so concerned. Bitch say Hi to your Lover! Bam, he hits her with her own phone. Speak now to this bitch or forever hold your piece.

Aaaaaaant!

London sit tight I'm on my way!

LONDON! Where is she? What the fuck have you done to her?

Nah my nigga, don't worry about her. Who you need to worry about is you right now!

Yeah okay what's good my nigga? Bam!

Ant jaws Sir straight in his mouth. Sir follows up and cracks Ant in his jaw. Both men put up a serious fight. Sir slams Ant on to the floor causing London's coffee table to shatter. As Sir attempts to stomp Ant, Ant sweeps Sir right off of his feet. Bam! Sir hits the floor hard; however busting his right temple open on the corner of the couch! Both men are bleeding at this time pretty badly.

Ssssstop it pppplease, London attempts to say while trying to stand up.

As both men see her laying hopelessly on the floor their rage for each other escalates. Ant attempts to go towards London than suddenly Bang! Shots were fired!

Everybody lay the fuck down. Nobody move and nobody will get hurt! You pay what you owe and I'll leave. You come up short or straight don't have my cash then ama kill the bitch! It's not personal Ant but you and yo brother was never gonna walk this town trying to walk the connect.

I been on yo heels for the last month and a half. When you came home I laid you out. First you started coming up short. Then transparent as hell. Well so you thought. This pretty lil woman right here must have some great pussy as I seen you here so much I thought you moved in.

Man kill that son of a bitch Sir yells out expressing his anger and jealousy.

And if I do young man what in the name of heaven do you think I'm going to do with you. Do you see these men? They're trained unlike you aimless fools claiming to be gangsters. Ya both bitches and coward ass mother fuckas. Now back to my bread do you have it son? All forty seven thousand you owe.

Aaaant London trys to shout out but to faint to say it. All of a sudden she spirals into a seizure episode needing medical attention. Sir knowing the medication she needs and what to do pleads with the man to help her. He does and gives Ant 24 hours to pay his debt!

Aye-yo I know what you're thinking, but it's not what you think. Trust me I got that man bread and he gon have it today! I put that on my deceased mom! Get London to the hospital and I'll take care of this nigga!

What! I mean what am I going to tell them happened to her? What if she remembers me and her fight and she tells on me?

Worry about that later. If you have any love for her do what's right!

191

**************Meanwhile****************

So you know Sir found out London was fucking Ant while he was up top!

What! Tea! Do spill it Sky! I know this is going to be good.

Well, Briyanna was at the cook-out and we all know that she want's on with Ant so bad it's crazy. Now her not knowing I want that nigga too, I dropped the dime to her. I figured if she snitched it I could move her out of the way and have her looking like a weak minded bitch. Therefore he would start kicking it back with me, feel me. I mean he did read me the last time we were together but as far as I'm concerned he worth it.

When I saw that man on stage at the cook-out my heart skipped a beat!

I feel you! He is that man, and fine as hell too!

True and I'm going to be in his life I promise you that. Just wait and see! I just hope.

You just hope what?

Nothing, nothing, nothing. I just will. You'll see!

Meanwhile Sir manages to get London to the hospital. Even with the possibility of it meaning he may go back to jail, he felt bad for what she was going through. He knew her mother was soon going to be on the scene. Now those two didn't get along so Sir was preparing himself to see her face to face.

Why is it every time you are around my daughter her life is endangered! What in the hell is wrong with you young man? What has my daughter done to you for you to treat such a beautiful spirit this way?

Ma'am!

Ma'am my ass, GET OUT! GET OUT RIGHT NOW! I can no longer stand the sight of you. I swear on my life should I find out you had anything to do with this I'll make sure you'll be pushing up daises myself! GET OUT!

Is everything okay in this room?

Yes doctor it is. I'm sorry!

Yeah it's okay, and I hope when yo daughter wake up she remembers that it was me who saved her life. Had she not been fucking with that hood nigga Ant she might not be in the shit she in now. Opps! Did I say that! Sir starts laughing. So you see ma'am. Ya daughter likes hood niggas and she was fucking this clown all while she was with me. I've learned a thing or two about old wise tales myself growing up. I mean you have heard of the saying "The apples don't fall to far from the tree haven't you"? If I were your husband I'd question your ass or maybe she gets it from her father as from what she shared with me he stayed cheating on your ass too! Have a great day and no matter what let London know I loved her!

Back in the streets Ant has business to attend to. Shit! Why did this fool come fa me so damn quick. I have to get this money right . I swear I hope my brother has his 25k or it's going to be problems.

Bzzzzzz. Bzzzzzzz. Bzzzzzz.

Text Message #1. Hey baby. I know your probably still angry at me but I miss you. Hit me back if you miss me to, and there is something I think you should know

Text #1 Reply. What up Sky. It's really not a good time, but what's up.

Text #2. Well miss you and what we had. I know you said II wouldn't be the one but I think different.

Text#2 reply. Sky I just said now isn't the time if that's all you were trying to say then I'll hit you back later.

Text #3. Well yes and no, but it sounds like this is really a bad time so ill text you later.

Text #3 reply. Kool

Text #4 (out going from Ant) Bro what up! Meet me on-stage (code for the their trap spot). It's a 911

Text #4 reply. I'm already here.

Thank God! I swear I hope he got me. I have to make sure London good and my rep. I told my brother not to play with this man money. Maybe that cook-out wasn't such a bright idea after all. I'm sure we spent 10k on that alone. What the Fuck! If I never needed you before God I need you right now!

194

Ring! Ring! Ring!

Hello!

Just so you know I meant every word I said. Oh girl's room number is 1355 private. I can and I will eliminate her at 12 am on the dot. Make sure you have all my cash, and not even a penny short! CLICK!

FUCK! WHAT THE HELL! I CAN'T LOSE LONDON DUE TO MY SILLINESS! Ant begins to tear while yelling storming out of the house. Ant couldn't wait to see his brother so he decided to call.

716-553-1213 Ring! Ring! Ring!

Bro!

What's good!

Ole-Boy came to see me about that bread. he said if we don't have it paid in full by midnight tonight he was going to off London.

He said what!

Bro you heard me! He said.... BOOM! Ant driving recklessly attempting to get to his brother ran a red light without notice. He instantly crashed into a street light pole trying avoid the cars coming in his direction. Hitting his head on the steering wheel knocked him out cold!

Bro! Bro! Bro! What's up? Bro! What's going on? What was that loud noise? Bro! I'm on my way! Ant's brother hangs up and instantly attempts to locate his brother via their locater installed application. While pulling up to the scene he sees the boys in blue and every medical team needed.

Damn near about to panic out of know where a very close friend who just so happened to be a nurse strolled up. Mickey he's going to be fine. Are you okay? Yes ummmm, I'm fine. Well you can follow us to the hospital or I can call you once we arrive. Mickey says call me. He hands his friend a stack and says take care of his car and him for me please. I'll be to the hospital shortly. I have something to deal with first!

Here! Here's yo mutha fuckin cash! All 47k. Not a dime missing or a penny short. We good?

We are! Oh and Hahahahahaha sorry to hear about your brother. I send my deepest sympathy. I hope when he gains consciousness from his coma, maybe we all can work together again! Hahahahaha! I bet next time you won't try and play a God!

******* Sadly 1 week Later ********

Ring! Ring! Ring!

Hello!

Hello may I speak to the emergency contact listed for London as Sissily?

This is I. How are you? Is my daughter okay? What's wrong?

Ma'am. As your daughter has been under our care for a while now. We have ran all types of test and X-Rays attempting to make sure we resolved any and all findings related to her injuries we found a major concern to be valid. We ran test this morning and and they were positive. I don't know how to say this ma'am but!

SAY WHAT? BUT WHAT? TELL ME! TELL ME RIGHT NOW PLEASE!

Ma'am. If you can come to the hospital I myself and three additional specialist would like to speak with you. Due to London's condition just now improving we agreed to tell her last. This diagnosis is going to be a real life changing event requiring supportive efforts from everyone around her.

My God is powerful! I rebuke what the devil has cast in the name of the Father, his son and the Holy Spirit!

Ma'am will you be on your way?

I will be there right away!

Oh and we may need information regarding any current relationships London may have been involved in! Thanks and we will discuss our findings soon.

Sissly tried hard to hide the hurt and pai, but she just couldn't. Her daughter was everything to her. Night after night she prayed for God to remedy this situation. Just when she was thinking things were improving now there's another situation to face. The fact that she even had to discuss her daughters past relationships started a internal rage. Sissily couldn't stand the sight of Nasir, and the fact that the devil hadn't reared his ugly head thus far was both a good and a bad thing. Meanwhile!

Hey bae! How are you?

I'm good now. That was one helluva night last night and I enjoyed myself with you. It's been a long time since I trusted someone and had someone make me feel this way about them.

That's good Nasir! I'm glad that I could do that for you. I'm really a different kind of female. I don't associate with females as they can't be trusted so you will see my click runs thin. Secondly I not the type of woman to do the "he say" "she say" thing. What we discuss stays between us. My family is small and I trust thinly.

Sounds like my kind of girl. Come over here and sit on it again for me.

Hahahaha! Nope! Not until you finally end what you have going on with ole-girl. You told me you had some-one when we first started fucking around. I mean grant it we were off and on so much you couldn't call what we had going on much of anything. Since you been home and we been chilling. This is what I want and from how things have been going. It appears to be what you want as well.

Yeah you right baby, and I think ama do that today! Now I tell you this. I was staying with her and my mom, but I been working on trying to get me my own place.

I know that it's hard when you touch down and baby I got you. My daughter grown so we won't ever need to worry about any confusion in my house. Just make sure that while you're staying with me, you don't bring anything uninvited or wanted with you when you come home.

What you mean about that?

STD's, Babies you don't already have, Nonsense, Bitches and the police!

Oh okay I got you! You good baby. I promise you that.

I hope so as I've been waiting on the exact moment when I could say and call you all mines.

Ring! Ring! Ring!

Hello!

Tashawn it's important!

What's wrong?

We have all been summons to attend a family meeting tonight! I'm not sure of all the details but it's mandatory.

Oh! Okay! Cool! Um well I'll be there and I hope that everything is alright!

You god bae?

Yeah I'm good. I just have to go to my aunt's tonight. I tell you what! In the meantime take my daughters key and go get you one made. She uses this one when she decides to come and spend some time with me. Grab your stuff and you can put it in the extra room for now. We will finalize what we doing later on this week.

Okay! Can you sit on it now?

Hahahaha, nope! I have to get ready to go. I have a lot to do before the family meeting. I tell you what I will do though.

What's that?

Put it in my mouth!

Yassssssssss mommy! Okay! I swear I love this girl!

Hello Ma'am!

Hello! What's wrong with my baby?

Well we found a blood clot on London's brain due to the inflammation of a superficial vein. The likeliness of this stems from a damaged vein due to a high trauma injury. That we will need further investigation on as to what caused this trauma. Secondly.

My God!

Are you okay Ma'am?

Yes!

Should I continue?

Yes!

Okay. Secondly we found her to be in need of Beta-agonist medication. This medication is needed to assist with re-opening London's air passages by relaxing her muscles. Her airways tightened and closed almost preventing her from breathing on her own. This was due to the shock of the trauma and the series of events happening within her body at the same time.

Lord please protect my baby!

And Lastly Ma'am.

Wait there's more?

Yes Ma'am. Lastly we found London to be in need of immediate treatment as she has stage 3 Breast Cancer!

Oh my Lord! Please give us all your strength!

Hey mom! How's London doing?

She's doing the best she can Nye. At this moment I feel like I'm losing my daughter. After she found out she was diagnosis with breast cancer, the look she gave was deadly. I'm about to go down stairs and get her up now. Today will be her first day of treatment. You should really come by, as I'm sure London would be happy to see you.

Well um honestly mom, I'm not ready to see my girl like that. I almost want to cry now talking about it. I have to get myself together because what I do know is my sister looks to me as her protector. If I break she is going to lose it! I'M SO FUCKING PISSED! Why did it have to be her mom? Why her? Anyone and I mean anyone who knows London knows she has the biggest heart you could ever imagine. Nye begins to cry harder.

I know baby, I know. Imagine how I feel. The kids have no clue. They just think mom is sick and she's here with me so I can take care of her. Her aunt is having a small gathering later to let a few of London's cousins know what's going and how they may be able to assist. You are more than welcome to attend if you would like.

Okay that sounds good mom! I really wish I had myself together, but mom this is really hard for me. I mean my girl is one of few who can wear her own hair and people still feel she has bundles in it. She has the prettiest smile, and her eyes are amazing.

Nye! Girl calm down. One things for certain is that my baby is blessed and well protected. Believe that! I've been praying in my prayer closet since we found out! I know she is going to be alright. I know (London's mom says faintly).

Grand ma! Mommy said to come here. She's throwing up. Yuck!

Okay Sincere. Tell her I'm on my way down stairs now. Nye I'll tell her you called to see how she was doing.

********** From London's Phone ***********

Text message #1) Hello!

Text message reply #1) What up?

Text message #2) Nothing. Not feeling to well since coming out of the hospital

Text message reply #2) Damn, you was in the hospital. What's wrong

Text message #3) Well I don't really know and am still unsure as to how I got there. All I can remember is you taking care of me.

Text message reply #3) Oh Yeah. You had, had a seizure.

Text message #4) Okay! I knew it had to be something. Well I have something to tell you.

Text message reply #4) Okay and so do I. Matter of fact let me go first. Due to you cheating on me with my man I no longer think we should be together!

Text Message #5) What! Wait! I mean you have been with everyone you could possibly be with except my family. You've embarrassed me, put me down, and given me nasty pussy diseases. I can't believe you!

Text Message reply #5) Oh well London. You should of thought about that before you started fucking my man.

Text Message #6) Sir I have Breast Cancer!

Text Message reply #6) Word! I'll pray for you. My girl want me to stop texting so I hope you get better. Bye!

London drops her phone and breaks down in tears. She instantly starts to feel guilty for being with Ant and wondering if she was being punished by God for not staying true to her belief and practices of loyalty, love and relationships.

Hey baby you okay in here? LONDON! BABY!

No! Nonononono! Call 911! Someone please call 911!
Baby everything is going to be okay! I promise you! Jesus he will fix it! Baby girl believe in it! Wake up! Believe in it!

Grand ma! What's wrong with mommy! Is mommy okay!

Operator on-call! Where about is the emergency?

1410 Eggertville Rd.

What's the emergency?

My daughter is unresponsive. Please help!

Okay ma'am. Emergency vehicles are on the way shortly. Can you please tell me what happened so we can better assist you?

Ummm I honestly don't know. My daughter was getting ready to go for her first Chemo appointment while I was upstairs getting ready. I heard a loud boom and when I came into her room it appeared she.

Ma'am?

It appeared she attempted to strangle herself! (Londons mom bursts out crying loudly). Please get someone here now! Please!

Mommy! Mommy! What's wrong mommy. Talk to me please.

(Suddenly) Cough, cough, cough.

Baby!

Cough, cough, cough.

Baby just stay with me. Please stay with me. Help is on its way! I promise you. Everything's gonna be alright! (Sissily begins to sing the old gospel hymn).

Bam, bam, bam! 911 let us in! Bam, bam, bam!

My mom is in the room with my grand ma to the right!

Okay thanks! Please step aside!

Okay response unit. Client is semi-responsive. A failed attempted suicide is the reason for assisted medical attention. Will provide oxygen and insert an I.V. "St. Joseph's Medical Treatment Center" is the request of the clients family for treatment. Ma'am will you be riding with us or following behind.

I will follow behind due to the kids. Thank you for arriving so soon.

That's my job ma'am. It's just a blessing this didn't work out the way she planned. Please be aware that due to this being an attempt of suicide it is highly likely she will be admitted to a mental health unit for psychological evaluation.

Dear, dear, dear. I'll continue to pray in the meantime as no one has the final says but God!

Hello and thank you all for coming over. I felt the need to speak to the family as a whole and discuss on behalf of my sister Sissily and niece London. Tashawna why you bring me here. It doesn't sound like this is going to be a good time to tell yo family I'm your man.

Boy shhhhh and be quite. Let's go have a seat in the front or you can stay in the back with my uncles and play that damn 2K16 on playstation.

Hahahaha! Girl you think you know me don't you! Muah they both share a kiss.

Let me go in here as I'm already late.

I received news that London was diagnosis with Breast Cancer earlier last week. Now to my surprise London attempted to take her own life a few days ago which caused for our family meeting to be slightly delayed. She successfully completed her first Chemo treatment today and is under careful watch at this time with her mom. In order for London to successfully beat this terrible disease, she is going to need every one of our participation. I did invite them to the meeting if London was feeling up to it, in an adverse effort to show her we are all fighting with and for her.

Hhhhello everyone. Thank you all for coming and wanting to offer me your support, but I am gracefully declining your assistance. At this time I am wishing to just fight and fight as hard as I can with and for those dearest to me. Now is not the time to vent or read anyone their rights, bu please understand where I am coming form. Not all prayer is good prayer and not all help is willing. That being said I will reach out to those I choose when I choose. Thank you! Cough, cough, cough!

Cuz are you okay? Tashawna asks.

Yes I'm fine. Thank you for asking. What brings you here, as I've not seen or heard from you since high school.

Well come in the kitchen with me. I want to share something with you. Do you want anything while we're in here?

Cough, cough, cough. No!

Well I know I haven't been around due to so much negative in my life, but girl God is amazing. Don't give up on anything just pray. God is so good. I made it through my storm and I know you can too. Bae! Come here. I want you to meet my cousin!

WHAT!

HELL NO!

Sky is excited after receiving a long awaited phone call. She jumps up to get dressed and off she went. How is he? Is everything okay? I came as soon as I was told he woke up!

Yes dear, Ant is doing well. Unfortunately there are so many people here to visit him, we are limiting visitation times by everyone. I know that you came and wanted to show your love and care, but it will be near impossible to see him today. Maybe you should come back in the morning. What's your name hun? Sky rolls her eyes when she sees Ant's ex Tamika going in before responding. My name is Sky!

Okay Sky! I'll make sure to tell him you came to see him.

This shit really has me pissed all the way off. I can't believe how that bitch made it up here switching and shit! That hoe done been around the block three times more than me. She must be broke, strolling in like he her man. Yeah Okay. I wonder how everyone going to feel when I tell him we're having a baby! 9 weeks to be exact! Thu!

(As Sky is walking out of the hospital she sees Ant's brother and immediately walks over to speak with him)

Hey there!

Hey what up? Sky right?

Right!

Okay! You been in to see Ant yet?

No! Unfortunately it was to crowed so I was told to come back tomorrow.

Nah! come back with me, I'm sure I can get you in real quick. I know my brother always had a mean fan club, but I know those he actually paid attention too as well.

Awwww! Seriously? Feeling like a winner she is ready to go in and see Ant now more than ever.

Yeah! I mean you and him may not have been in a relationship but he appreciated ya company feel me. I mean you understood what you two had right?

(Sky now looks of defeat. Just as soon as she thought she was getting somewhere again she was put down, then bling! Sky congers up an idea and is almost sure it will be a winner)

Yeah I knew exactly what was going on and how he felt about me for facts. I mean yeah we were friends, but somewhere someway somehow this happened. Sky pulls out her sonogram picture.

What the? Who? Wait! Huh? You mean to tell me your pregnant by my brother? Fuck outta here! Hell yeah you going in! Come on. Come with me now!

Sky begins to smile as her plan worked perfectly!

Chapter 7

"Brewing Karma"

So I take you too know each other?

Man get me the fuck out of here. I'm not trying to be around this nonsense.

Nonsense? Nasir what the fuck, cough, cough, cough is that supposed to mean? You wasn't saying all that when you came home and was telling me how much you loved me and wanted to make things right, now was you? Don't lie either!

Maybe, but that was until you fucked my man Ant!

What! Wait! You too! Jail and make it right! Nasir you have some explaining to do.

Man bae it's all good. She is who I was with, but I choose you!

Man this is my cousin. Right now she don't need to be going through this type of shit. That's not only fucked up on her behalf, but mines as well. I swear I didn't know anything about you and him. What's even more crazy is the fact that I saw your name and number in his phone and text messages. I would have never thought this was you.

Typical Sir. You know what? I don't even care! I'm glad you too have each other. Cough, cough, cough. (London begins to feel weak trembling and spits up).

Cousin! I got you. Fuck what's going on. I'm never going to be with no man that does this shit to women! Nasir go ahead with that shit. I'm done!

Oh so you just going to kick me the fuck out, then fuck you bitch!

London come on. This nigga got it twisted. We a family my nigga!

Man fuck both yal bitches!

Excuse me mister! Who are you? We don't do that in this house!

Lord I rebuke the devil. This boy here has been nothing but problems sister. He has done my dear London so wrong that it has taken everything from me not to kill him myself. Lord forgive me!

Tashawna who is this?

Auntie he was my boyfriend until I found out he was London's man prior.

Oh Jesus help me! Boom (Sissily grabs a brown coffee mug from off of the counter and throws it at Nasir, attempting to knock his head off).

Bitch is you crazy! That's it I'm outta here.

Sissily are you okay? Tashawna get that mother fucker out of here and don't ever bring him here again!

Oh ma'am you don't have to worry. I would honor your request with a heartbeat Ma'am, as I didn't want to come here no way.

Bam! London hits the floor causing everyone to stare as she passes
out from all the negative energy and being overwhelmed. Today
she had just taken her first Chemo treatment and was completely
weary and exhausted. Sir looks over and almost runs to her, but
allows his pride to take him and he storms out of the house.

Call 911!

Hey baby!

Umm. Ant grunts while turning over in his bed and waking up.
Breath mildly tart as his mouth is bitter and dry. Sky can see it as
his lips are chapped and pealed. Hey! What are you doing here so
late.

Well your brother was going to get me in but the nurses said you
needed rest and asked that everyone leave out. As I was leaving
my girl who works here told me to hide out in one of her patients
rooms. After knowing everything that you went through in that car
accident and seeing this (Sky takes out her sonogram picture to
show Ant that he would be a father) she helped me get in here with
you. I wanted to be the first person you seen as soon as you woke
up. I wanted you to know that I was going to be here with you
through thick and thin. Good and bad.

Wow! I honestly don't know what to say. Can you hand me my
mouth sponge, tooth brush, basin, and toothpaste. Oh can you put a
little water in it for me?

Sure, and you could start of by saying your happy at least. I mean
you haven't shared much with me about your daughter but I saw
her mother yesterday when she came to see you.

Oh yeah you did. She wants us to get back together. She thinks it would be good for our daughter.

Well what do you think? I mean I am having a baby by you now as well.

True but why would you have a baby by someone who doesn't even love you. Sky we cool and I do and have appreciated the time we spent but I don't want to be with you. Should you decide to keep the kid then I just have to do what any real nigga would do.

WOW! I can't believe this. Well it's cool Ant, and just so you know I am having the baby. You want a blood test after, than that can happen too. Just know I came to you like a women and in hopes that you would give me an opportunity to be the woman you search so hard for.

Well I honestly came to you like a man and acknowledged my situation. I accepted my responsibilities. You know just like I told my daughters mother where my heart is. Until I can find a women with as much heart, grace, and beauty as London I'll just play the field.

WHAT! Well that bitch has Breast Cancer. While you playing the field you better pray that bitch survive it! Thu!

What you mean she has Breast Cancer? Who told you that? Where is she? My God I need to talk to her.

 Pissed about having again to go back to his mother's house, Sir knew that it would only be a matter of time before he had to address the situation with London. He knew both his mother and sister cared deeply for her, and having to tell them the truth was going to be difficult.

What the fuck is you out here doing my nigga? Like London has been there for you from everything you could possibly imagine. How in the hell you knew she had Breast Cancer and didn't tell me or mommy! I found out when I was getting off of work. They had me in the ER and when the chart came in and I read the name I almost passed out. You a bitch you know that. I'm telling mommy and I'll be going to see her too by the way.

Jazz chill. Why you always hopping on shit with me. Like it's always my fault, but I bet you ain't know she fucked my man Ant did you?

Ha, I did, and so the fuck what! You done put your nasty little penis in everything moving. Care? Nope I do not. I guess it isn't any fun when the rabbit has the gun is it? Fuck out of here! You have done that girl absolutely wrong. I'm amazed she didn't stay with Ant! He was nothing but a gentleman to her.

CRACK! (Sir breaks the glass he was just drinking water out of with his right hand causing it to bleed like crazy).

And! So what you mad for? Nasir you need to pray to God for forgiveness. Mommy told me what you said to her as well. Karma is a bitch. Watch what you put out here in this world. When it comes back baby, you may not be able to handle its' presentation.

Yeah okay! You always trying to talk to me like I ain't shit! You should have told your mother to watch what she put out in this universe. She made it hard for all of us. We all were three seconds from being put into foster home if it wasn't for me risking my life stealing food, robbing niggas, hustling as much as I could afford too and bunking crack heads with fake dope to get us something to eat. I could have been killed multiple times. Not to mention I couldn't even bring my work home because she smoked up all my dope and didn't give a fuck how I paid the plug back. Left me in a hot ass mess, but I managed. When I went to jail at 14 and no one came to see me or offered to send me a package fucked me up. So if you think I honestly give a fuck about how mommy feel. I don't. You might be younger than me, but I have always looked up to you. I always wanted better for you.

Well you need Jesus Nasir. It's time for you to forgive others and yourself. Until you do that you will only set yourself up to miss your blessings. Was our mom perfect? No! She had a man just like the one you have grown to become. Mommy worked 4 jobs at times to take care of us. It wasn't until she met a man much of like who you have become who drove her to the point of no return. I prayed for mommy Sir while I cried. I forgave her for trying then and I forgive her still now. What she did to herself and her children made me a better women. What she did as a woman and mother should make you a better father and man. I'm just saying!

Okay sis! I'll talk to you later. Sir walks to the bathroom as tears of pain start to fall down his face. His freshly cut and trimmed mustache now obtained heavy snot. His 300 pound ass fell to his knees at the bathroom sink asking God why did he make him this way. Lord I know what I do is not to your liking or discretion, but I do believe it isn't my fault. I want to love and trust I really do, but how can I, when all I have endured has been hurt, trauma and pain. Lord I know I'm not right and I do a lot of wrong but please if you can spare London's life for me. I am not for her and I see that now more than ever. I am scared of losing her. Please ask her to find it in her heart to forgive me, but I am not man enough to wake up and find her unresponsive. I'd rather walk away then be where I know I should be.

Bro! I need you to come up to the hospital and see me quickly!

Ant what's wrong you good? Do I need to come strapped? What you saying?

No! None of that. Bring my cell phone too with you when you come. That bitch Sky just left from up here talking about she was going to have my baby and told me fuck London because she has Breast Cancer damn near all in the same breath.

WORD?

WORD!

Okay I'll be there in a minute. Meanwhile you need me to bring you something up there.

Hell yeah. Grab me a "Labatts" a good cold one. I don't give a fuck what these doctors in here are saying. It's already bad enough I can smoke nothing. I bet I sip on a cold one.

Okay got you! Be there in a few!

Damn Lord (Ant begins to talk out loud while lying in the bed with his hospital gown on, both legs with braces as he still has a corrective paralysis to both legs) please save my queen. If only I could go and see her I would. I swear I'll do whatever you ask of me to help her fight this. That girl needs a break and I need her. Lord please I beg of you to give me the strength needed to get my queen. I know deep in my heart that she is for me as I am for her. In due time I'm sure she will realize what we shared was more than momentary. It was designed for a life time.

(Ant suddenly nods off while awaiting his brothers arrival until he feels a warm, soft and wet feeling on his fingertips)

Hello Ant! How is your day my handsome patient?

Ma'am! You know you could get in trouble for this?

Yeah, but who's going to tell? I've watched you since you came into this hospital. I've taken better care of you than any of the women I've seen come in to visit you. With that being said I know everything that I need to know and that's you have no one in your life right now that you need and want. I'm sure I can be that and more.

How is that when you all you have offered me is your wet ass pussy juices on my fingertips! I mean don't get me wrong you are right about a lot of shit, but right now I'm happily single. Oh Shit! (Suddenly while Ant was speaking Nurse Rhonda slide under the sheets and began to pleasure him orally.)

Ohhhh! SHIT! What the? Damn! Baby ama get myself in a lot of trouble in here. Wait! I think your raping me! Are you? Ooooooooooooh! I'm about to cum!

I swallow so go ahead!

(In comes Ant's brother) Pimpin! What's good? You look a little flushed.

Man did you bring me that drink, cause Lord knows I need it now for-real.

(Nurse Rhonda walks out with her uniform dress half buttoned and pretty pink lipstick perfectly placed on her voluptuous lips, subliminally teasing anyone who starred long enough) Hello!

Hhhhhi! Damn bro I'd never come home if she was taking care of me!

Well bro give me your strength and you can lay here all you want. Look I need you to check on London for me. Get her three dozen roses. One has to be Pink, another white, and the last yellow. Make sure they accompany a teddy bear that's human size almost. No need to write anything. When you deliver it she will know where it came from. Just tell her I'm praying for her and I'm here when she needs me.

Damn London has you sprung! No wonder you and Sir was beefing over that broad.

Broad she will never be. I hope in due time she will be my wife.

What about that girl with the baby?

Right! Honestly I don't know where I stand with London anyways. I'm just man enough to make an attempt. She may even have gone back to fucking with that nigga Sir. Bitch ass!

Well I'll take care of that for you right away. Let me get out of here as I have to pick the twins up from school.

Okay! Tel my niece and my nephew uncle Ant says he will be home soon and I love them.

Will do. Get some rest. I'll holla at you soon!

One!

Two!

Sissily was by her daughters side from dusk to dawn most days, while still managing to be a great wife, and awesome grandmother. She awoke daily to her same routine; however, today she planned on having a talk with God hoping to obtain peace.

Yet another long day! Lord give me the strength I need to fight this deadly disease with and for my baby. As I sit here and watch her sleep, I can see the hurt, struggle and pain. I remember when it made her happy helping people. She stayed convincing me that everyone deserves to live a happy life. I stopped judging a lot of people all because of her.

Ummm, excuse me and hello! Did I come at a bad time? My name is Jazz and I am a great friend to London. She has helped me in every time of need I've ever been in, so it is only right that I return the favor.

Well Jazz yes, I can tell you know my baby all too well; however, I need to know you are here with good will and intentions. So many people have been hurtful and done harm that I cannot allow or stand for anything more to hurt her. We've been in the hospital so much this last month and a half that I'm starting to believe they have a room with her name on the door. Sissily giggles just a bit putting an expression of hope back in her spirit and joy in her heart.

Well ma'am I can only show you. I work here. I promise you. Nothing will hurt or harm my friend, cousin, auntie, sister. She has played so many roles in my life since I was 9 I wouldn't know what to tell you. I'll make sure she's clean, she eats, she prays and gets her strength back. You don't believe me just watch.

 When you can't I can. I'm stepping up to fill that void. Her son and her daughter need you as you need you too. I will do my best and I promise you that.

Well you sound very assuring about this.

Yes ma'am I am. I just stopped in to check on her before I clocked in for over-time. I'll be back in a few as luckily I'll be the nurse assigned to her unit tonight anyhow.

Wow! What a blessing. Maybe when you come in I'll go home and take care of my grandkids. I'm sure they are again worried and hungry. Hahahaha!

No problem. I am a woman of my word and I promise you I'll be right here! Jazz leaves out of London's room in a hurry attempting to hide the hurt and pain she began to feel after seeing London say so peacefully but frowned sleeping. As Jazz wipes her eyes attempting to keep her freshly installed lashes on, she bumps into Ant's brother.

Aye pretty lady, I didn't know you worked here?

And I didn't know you needed too, what up?

Okay! No need to be so tight! Relax. You want me to rub your feet later?

No! What I want you to do is stop aggravating me. You see I'm not me right now I'm sure. Hell I can feel it, so I know you see it.

Yeah I do. I sincerely apologize. What's wrong? If you don't mind me asking.

I just saw London.

Yo brother girl London?

Yeah and they aren't together any more, thank God!

Okay. Well you know Ant here too.

No I didn't know.

Yeah he just told me to check on her too. Yo do me a favor. Let me know if they plan on discharging her tomorrow or not. If not I'll bring her gifts here for her from him.

Gifts?

Yeah. I don't know what she did to my right-hand but ugh, he love that girl man. Can I sneak a peek. I'm sure he wants to know how she is doing.

Well her mom is in there with her now but you can look through the peak hole.

Damn! Yo is she going to be alright? She doesn't look to good laying there.

Well from what I do know her charts are saying her body is rejecting the treatment she is undergoing. They may have to keep her as that's a major problem if she can't take the medication prescribed. London could die if the doctors can't treat it fast enough.

Damn!

Right!

As Mikey walked away he was thinking how he was going to tell his brother what he just saw. London didn't look good and he definitely didn't want to be the one to tell him

Bzzzzzz, bzzzzz, bzzzzz.

Tashawna reaches to check her phone.

Text #1) What up?

Text#2) WYD?

Text #1 reply) Sir you ain't shit. I can't believe how disrespectful you were to my family and my cousin when she didn't need to be exposed to such nonsense.

Text #3) Man fuck all that. Real talk is I miss and love you. I prayed for her recovery but I can't help where my heart is. Like she might not make it. Maybe that's why God gave me you!

Text #3 reply) Fuck you mean Sir. She might make it too. I hope at least. Tashawna begins to think to herself maybe God did put us together. The circumstances are completely a mess, but I prayed for my man and he is who he sent. Hmmmmmm.

Text #4 from Tashawna) You may be slightly right. I mean this is fucked up. I feel bad but I love you too at the same damn time.

Text #5) Come get me yo!

Text #5 reply) Where you at Sir?

Text #6) My mom's

Text #6 reply) Okay I'm on my way

Tashawna lays her phone on her marble top counter in the kitchen. While running her hands in her hair trying to fix it and make it sexy she begins to think out loud) Lord I do hope that you will forgive me, but I had no idea they were together. I've loved him as he has loved me. I've met sisters and his step mother.

This I'm sure will be an honor to meet his biological mother. If Nasir didn't care he wouldn't have contacted me or as wrong as it was attempted to show me he is choosing me. I don't know what's going on right now, but for the most part I'm no fool. Sir does love me and he shows me. I'm sorry it was my cousin, but shit happens!

Tashawna grabs the keys to her mother's Chrysler and walks out of her apartment feeling sexy, accomplished, and ready for the world. Her hair swung down long with a bright red tint. She wore a fitted pair of jeans to show her curves and a white tank. Her favorite smell-good combination "Gucci Guilty" and "Victoria Secrets eavenly". She has worn that since the day she first had passionate sex with Nasir. It was something about that smell that always sent him on a passionate rage sexually with them. Tashawna knew the love they would make tonight would be everything and the signature to their destiny.

Beeeeeeeep! Code Blue room 1436 STAT!
Code Blue STAT, I repeat! Code Blue STAT!

OMG! That's London's room! Move!

Jazz slow down you okay? Jazz! Jazz! Jazz!

LONDON! NOOOOOOOOOOOOOOOO!
CALL HER MOM NOW! RIGHT NOW!
COME ON BABY YOU GOT THIS! I GOT YOU! PULL THE FUCK THROUGH LONDON COME ON! (London takes an allergic reaction to the new chemo drug they attempted to administer her. London's life slips away, but with prompt medical attention she was able to be revived.

Now in a medically induced coma, London lays still in her bed. Her beautiful faced expressed worry, fear, and confusion. Her beautiful smile was now silenced and frozen. She appeared limp, lifeless and spiritless).

My God! (London's mom Sissily drops to her knees alongside London's bed) As thankful as I am for you sparing my child's life once again and hearing our prayers, Lord I ask what is it you are using her to do? My nerves are discombobulated. I myself can't eat, sleep, or anything without worry. You are a trusting God and this I know, but your presentations are strong and I am yet confused.

Ma'am do you need anything? Jazz enters the room, eyes swollen and red from tears and fear.

No baby, I am fine. Thank you for gaining the strength to call me. I heard the scare and fear all in your voice. Just in that confirmed o me you are true.

Ma'am (Jazz attempts to speak while breaking down uncontrollably. Snot dripping out of her nose, makeup smeared, with puffy eyelids expressing the fear she felt and witnessed) Shhhhe, Shhhhhe almost left us (Jazz continues to cry hysterically).

Yes baby I know. Trust me I understand your tears as I've cried them so much I'm numb. We have to continue to pray and protect her as much as we can. God is watching and he hears us. I ask him all the time what is he using London for. Whatever it is it will be great. Her job isn't done yet! She has not found her purpose in life directed by our God. He has a plan and I know she I'll execute it royally when found.

Ma'am I am so sorry for losing it. I apologize as I know it is and was unprofessional but I was not allowing no other nurse to be in there without me. I made a promise to you, London and God that I would be there and I am. I felt like they were going to have to kill me if they let her die!

I know baby and it is okay now. Go and dry your eyes and clean your face. I'll be here for the rest of the night.

Knock, Knock, Knock!

Hello! Who goes there?

Delivery for London!

Delivery for London?

Yes Ma'am.

Come in.

Hello Ma'am. These are from my brother Ant. He would like to send his deepest regards to London's situation. He told me to tell her he sends his love and that he hopes when he can walk again they can pick up here they left off.

Who is this Ant you speak of young man, and why can't he walk? What are you street hoods who could only endanger my daughter's life more than it already is. From the looks of your clothes and that God awful smell you have I pray she awakes with a better mind and intention. Uhh!

Ma'am. I do apologize for my unlikeliness to you, but London is very fortunate to have you here by her side. See my brother and I lost our parents at the age of 13 and 10. We didn't want to go to foster care so we ran away. By the grace of God when he turned 16 he was able to become an emancipated minor. Under the careful eye of neighbor we stayed together. Now street wise yes that's how we had to eat and pay our bills, but these same streets also paid for both my brother and I to obtain college degrees debt free. My brother was in a bad car accident and just awoke from a coma days ago. So you see ma'am God isn't judging and neither should you. Now I'll leave these gifts here. If you don't mind he asked me to whisper something in her ear

No go ahead, and I am sorry young man. I know my daughter would be upset with me if she had heard me speak in that content, but she is my only daughter and I don't know what I would do without her.

Mikey walks over in his baggy Levis jeans, All white Polo shirt with a fresh pair of all white Air Max "95" on his feet. He smelled of weed strongly mixed with Fahrenheit cologne. His walk was slow and stiff with a mild limp. He had a fresh crisp edge up with a large diamond earring in his left ear.

London (he whispers). Ant says he loves you and that when you wake up and beat this he will be right here standing tall waiting to take you home. My brother loves you. I'll be praying for you as well. In the meantime as a symbol of his love he asked me to place this on your finger. Ma'am (he speaks up and looks in a seductive way at London's mom) Can you come over here please.

Um yeah, sure!

My brother would like for someone dear and close to be a witness to this.

Wait! (A loud voice says from the entrance to London's room, from a man in a wheel chair and hospital gown in much need of a haircut, being pushed by Nurse Jazz)

Ant! How did.

I told him I saw you go in with the flowers as I had to wok his floor today. After I shared minimal information he demanded I bring him here to see her! Ms. Sissily if you trust me and wouldn't mind, I believe this could be really good for her.

Oh, okay!

London baby I love you! My heart you have. My soul isn't complete without you. I need for you to pull through. I promise you I'm going to get myself in order to be everything that you ask me to be. I'm going to work out until I can walk again. I'm going to get down here every day until you wake up and say hi to me. I am going to make you my wife and have a happy family with you,

What?

Ma'am shhhh! This is getting good!

Until I can protect you the way a real man should I have prayed and asked God to order my steps. With this promise ring I place on your hand I give you my love and promise to be your protector. If this isn't what you want, I will be hurt, but I will also understand. I love you London and will be right here waiting on you to return back to me.

**************Two Weeks Later!************

Bae? Sooooo, from what it appears like to me is that we have moved in together. With that being said, what do you plan to pay on my rent and bill expenses?

What? Do I look like I have a job or something. You see me bust a move every here and there. You know I'm not working and I have two kids to take care of.

Well I understand, but you are going to have to look for something or bust a move some way to help out here. I am already breaking the lease by having you stay here. When they find out I'm sure it will be an additional expense to my rent. Not to mention when are you going to change your parole address to here?

What! Like seriously! Do you hear all of the shit you asking me. A man hasn't even been here 30 mutha fucking days and you already pushing me to go back where the fuck I came from.

Oh so you could help London but you couldn't do shit for me huh?

AWW hell nah! That's it! That is it, that is it, that is it! You done fucked me up all the way right there. That's one thing I can say is that London never fucked with me on no control type shit. She knew a nigga was fucked up and continued to do what she been was doing. She told me that her mother raised her to be able to do shit on her own, so that no man could ever say he made her. She also said that anything a man could do would always be just a bonus, because she would have her back before anyone else could. Damn I miss her.

What! Oh you fucking miss her after all I been through with you. She fucking sick lying in the damn hospital and you would choose her over me!

She still in the hospital? What's wrong yo?

Go find out your damn self and leave my keys on the table in the process! So you just going to leave me like that (Tashawna questions Sir as he begins to pack his belongings, grabbing boxes and trash bags to help him store his things)?

Hell yeah! Like what part didn't you understand when I said what the fuck I said the first fucking time. Bitch you got me twisted. Now cause I moved in you want prompt payments of bills and shit! You wasn't worried about what I could bring to the table when I stuffing this fat ass dick up in yo pussy, now was you? You wasn't looking for no money when you was begging me to come over and spend the night was you? Hell since we making request and telling truth's you can't even cook for-real and ya head wack! Shit that's two qualities a bitch need right there to keep a man. I swear I made a big mistake!

Fuck you mean you made a big mistake? You not going to keep bringing up London to me either!

I know, that's why I'm leaving duh!

Matter of fact you ain't going nowhere! Fuck that! You said you loved me! You said it was me that you wanted to be with! You told me I was the one for you, so why all of a sudden you have such a change of heart? This must have been how you were truly feeling in the first place. I hate you! Get out!

Bye! (Nasir walks out of the house with bags being thrown behind him. Cracking up laughing talking shit) I hope you don't think you hurting me in any way. Like I don't need you! You just making it clearer for me to see why I made the mistake I did. I hope London can forgive me!

Boom! (A bag of Nasir's clothes hit him in the back of his head as he turned around to open the cab door) Look you better quit playing with me! I swear on everything I love, you fuck around and hit me again, you'll wish you had missed me.

GET OUT! DON'T CALL ME! DON'T COME LOOKING FOR ME, JUST LET ME BE!!!!!!!!!

You the one still talking. I'm trying to leave in peace. Thank you for helping me. I got this, and I am gone. (Suddenly Tashawna burst out in tears and runs into her room. Throwing herself on top of her king size bed yelling to God about how she feels)

WHY GOD WHY? I prayed. I read every passage in the bible. I've disassociated myself with my old ways and tribes. Was he a wolf in sheep's clothing? Did I make too much of the situation. I knew what I was doing when we were just so-called friends. I know that it was wrong to go back on my word about dealing with him, but I fell in love with him. I can't help how I felt and if he was choosing why not. Did I push him away? Was I wrong to question?

I'll be here every day until you wake up and that's a promise. It's been a week and so far I've managed to get enough strength to use a walker to get around. I know you hear me London. Come on baby girl. I need you to get better, so that we can leave out of here together. Say something London! Talk to me please! Man fuck the wedding. We can go to the justice of the peace as soon as you can leave. I just want you London baby please!

Ant places his head down in-between London's arms and just cries. While crying he starts to flash back about the life he had as a kid. Remembering what it was like having his mom. Anthony! A soft sweet voice cries out. Anthony again the voice cries out. Slowly lifting his head from London's arm a bright reflection appears walking towards the both of them. Anthony Lamar Jackson the image speaks Ant's whole name. You look as if you are afraid. I know you are afraid son, but trust me she will be fine. I'm proud of the man you have become, as I have watched carefully over you. She loves you, but there is much healing that needs to be done. I cannot promise you the outcome as there is much work to be done. Just know God only gives his hardest battles to his strongest warriors. I love you son and I am so proud of you!

Mom! (Ant shouts out trying to keep her with him) Mom, don't go, please mom I need you! (Ant cries out loud making an adverse attempt to get up and walk to her but falls down hard on to the hospital floor, knocking over the IV cart alongside London's bed).

Is everyone okay in here?

HELP!

MAN DOWN!

I'm okay, I'm okay! I just need. OUCH!

What's wrong?

Cough, Cough, Cough. Beeeeeeeeeep, Beeeeeeeeep!

Stat! Assistance in room #1436 prompt!

Is he okay?

Don't worry about me get Lonodn!

Breath! 1-2-3! Breath! 1-2-3!

Cough, cough, cough! Hhhhhhhhelp! Cough, cough, cough!

We're here London! God is so amazing we're here. Doctors all stand crowded around London's bed in full amazement as she has finally awoke. Doctors also noticed the rather large mass once highly noticeable on London's left breast was significantly smaller. This is great news. Someone call her mother as I am sure she would be happy to know London has waken!

Thanks mommy Ant says quietly as he remembers how beautiful she looked when she appeared. Every word she said he mentally tucked in his head, as aides assisted with getting him up and into a wheel chair. He didn't beg to stay either as he knew London needed rest. He also didn't want to stay, as he knew his battles were just beginning.

And now again for the third time. Nasir returns to the only place he has to go and that's moms. Hey sis! (Nasir says dragging it out, looking silly in an attempt to get on his sister Jazz good side)

Hey! What you want?

Aww sissy. Why do it have to be like that? I love you! Give me a kiss! (Sir leans in to kiss Jazz on her cheek)

Boy please! I don't know where them nasty, blunt crusted lips been. For all I know you have herpes!

See sis! Man, how's London?

Oh she's good. She's real good. Ant confessed his love to her, and put a promise ring on her finger. He really Loves her. I'm so happy for them!

Hahahaha! What you trying to make me jealous aren't you? Well ya not! Hahahahaha! I bet she don't even know it's on her finger. I called up to check on her though. They told me she wasn't accepting calls and limited visitors. Her condition has improved, but not yet into a full recovery. That's why I need you sis. I need to see her, and I know for a thousand facts her mother not letting me nowhere near her.

Facts! Hell I wouldn't let you near a roach, with your grimey ass. You got me twisted. Team London all day. We're only related by blood. London is my sister no matter what yal go through and I will always have her back.

So you not going to help me huh?

Why? Don't you think you've caused that girl enough grief already. Like seriously.

Maybe!

Do you honestly think this would be a good time to see her. I mean she is basically still trying to fight for her life. Like come on!

Yeah I guess so. I just want to right my wrongs and tell her I'm sorry. I'm happy for both Ant and her. I guess!

Yeah fucking right. You know deep down you mad as hell. Wait! Wasn't you just messing around with London's suspected cousin?

Suspected! What you mean about that?

Dude they was only cousins because their fathers were cool. Like real cool. You know how Ti-Ti is with us.

WORD!!!!!

Don't get any ideas. You was still wrong. You and her dumb ass.

I know right! Well I just want to say I'm sorry to her, meanwhile I'll lay right here and catch a few winks till it's time for you to go.

Hello my queen. I see your resting easy. Ant bends over and lays a kiss softly on London's cheek. Sissily, London's mom gracefully sits in her chair secretly admiring Ant's compassion and composure. Ant appeared to have just received a fresh shave and haircut. He was nicely dressed to have been still in the hospital.

Then!

Knock, knock, knock!

Hello Ms. Sissily, how are you and London?

Ant raises his head as that voice is all too familiar. Seeing Sky standing there with her stomach starting to poke out, he silently prayed to himself.

She's pushing through Sky. How are you? I see your doing well as you come bearing gifts. How far long are you?

Awww Ms. Sissily I'm close to 5 months now. I just found out what I was having today. I was on my way to show my son's father, but it appeared he wasn't in his room, so I stopped down to show some love and.

Wow! Congratulations Sky! Ant interrupts her trying to avoid a conflict and hide his happiness about having a son. Ms. Sissily I'm sorry to have to leave so soon as it is always a pleasure to see you when I stop in; however, I have therapy shortly so I'll be heading back up to my room.

Well okay son. Sure! You keep pushing. I'm happy you and London are both progressing.

Son! Oh! Okay, well I guess I'll be heading out too, as I want to go tell my son's father the great news!

Yes, yes. yes, my dear. Stop in anytime. I'm sure London would love to see you. I miss you all hanging out so much. It was beautiful seeing you Sky!

It was beautiful seeing you too, ma'am.

So you son now huh? Damn I thought maybe the streets might be lying a little bit when I heard you conveyed your love for London in all but, damn! I done seen it all. She laying up looking dead as hell with a ring. Her mama calling you her son, and here I am almost 5 months, fine as hell carrying your first son! (Sky takes the sonogram pictures out of her bag and throws them in Ant's face)

London, I mean Sky!

Damn you that sprung? You that in love. Fuck you! You know what, I'm tired of trying. You have said everything you could to hurt me and push me away, but no I still stayed true. I know my past isn't perfect, but who's is. Sky starts to cry as she thought showing Ant their baby boy might persuade him to come back to her.

Ant puts his head down trying to figure out where these feelings were coming from. Sky was looking so pretty. She wore a long fitted, t-shirt like dress that shaped her shape in every way.

 Her hair was hanging down long, straight, jet-black with a side part. She smelled like a flower garden. Sweet innocent and fresh. Her nails and toes were freshly painted and her glow was of the sun. Strangely she reminded him of when his mother came to him. Sky I'm sorry. Please come here. I mean I don't know what to do right now okay. You know how I feel about London, but you to have a special place in my heart.

Sky lifts her head and says: I do!

Yes you do! It was easy to hide it until now. Standing here seeing you with my child and how pretty you look, does make me question if what I did, I was supposed to do. I just want London to be okay as she has been through so much you know.

I know, but we all have in some way or another wanted what was best for someone. Look you can have. Ant silences Sky by pulling her close and kissing her on her lips. Suddenly a soft gentle kiss turns into an erotic tongue filled kiss. Walking by Sir sees them kissing.

Jazz, Jazz (sir says trying to whisper) you see this? I thought that nigga was trying to do right!

Damn! Me to bro! Now this some fuck shit right here. I can't believe this shit! Matter of fact (Jazz burst in Ant's room surprisingly interrupting the kiss). Yo what type of shit is this?

Yo chill Jazz!

Chill Jazz my ass Ant, what it do? Sir starts grinning so hard his cheeks looked like swollen cinnamon rolls.

What the fuck you doing here anyway Nasir?

Watching you get busted, from the looks of it! Hahahaha

He really left me, Tashawna says quietly to herself. It's been three days and he hasn't even texted me once. I call, straight to voicemail I go! I text, and I don't receive a response. Ughhhhhh! What the hell am I going to do? One part of me loves him and want's him back dearly; however, the other part of me has me mad as fuck for making me look stupid. I can't do this to myself anymore. I just can't. Why are you doing this shit to me Nasir. Why?

Ring, ring, ring.

Hello?

Girl what's up?

Shit, just laying on my bed staring at the damn wall, trying to get myself together.

Well I could get in trouble for this (Tashawna's friend Stacey who works at the hospital decides to call) but guess who has the mother fucking tea!

Girl who?

Girl me! Why I saw Ant in London's room and Sky. Now you know Ant gave London a promise ring, why the streets keep saying he proposed to her, and Sky is pregnant by Ant! 5 months girl, they having a boy!

Damn! How you find out all of that. I do work at the hospital, duh! Plus I was on the other side of the room with my patient. Since

London improved they moved her on a regular floor and she has a roommate.

Damn! Well girl you know I'm going to ask you, since you working getting all the damn tea.

Ask me what?

You haven't seen Nasir ass up there have you?

Oh hell no! Girl. I know that's your man and all that but the only way Nasir coming to the hospital is when

When what? Hello. Stacey! Stacey! Hello?

Ummm girl.

What?

The devil just walked in!

So what now? I mean this wasn't supposed to happen or maybe it was I don't even really know myself as I stand here. Ant looks down at his fresh out of the box all red "ADIDAS". As he stands tall with the sweat suit to match, the fresh scent of "Usher" cologne and crisp white tee his face expresses shame.

Damn Ant that's fucked up! I was really rooting for you! Shit you just as bad as my brother right now, and you (Jazz point's her finger and places it dead in the middle of Sky's brow) bitch need yo ass popped one good time!

Bitch please! Sky replies while smacking Jazz's finger from off her brow!

Bitch please what? What you going to do? Bust a grape one time before you attempt to come for me. We both know that had you not been pregnant, I probably would have thrown your ass out the window, so please don't tempt me. A double homicide is possible!

Come on Jazz, chill! Sky just chill out right now. I need to get my head together. I fucked up! I mean what yal want me to do? Hell she probably has no clue that I promised her my love anyhow. I do love her, and that's a fact, but I am also about to have a baby with someone I jive care for too!

And yal always talking about me! (Sir chimes in while sitting in the recliner by the window in the hospital room, wearing two day old jeans, a stained navy blue shirt that appeared to go with the jeans, smelling like stale cigarette's, eating a "Twix".)

Shut up Sir, Ant and Sky all said at the same time.

Man is her mom still in the room or did she leave out yet, Ant asked.

She left. She always leaves around 4, as she has to pick the kids up from their after school programs.

That is right. Well I tell yal what. Let me and Sir go in and visit with her. Sky you can either go home and I'll see you when I leave or you can wait here with Jazz.

I'll stay right here and wait for you. As a matter of fact, Jazz you do work here right? Could you check and see what's the hold up on my man's discharge papers? Please and thank you!

Ant you better get this bitch. Don't ask me shit, if you come back and this hoe missing you already know what happened.

Hey my Queen! How are you feeling today?

Hey my love, I've been waiting on you! What took you so long to come see me Sir? I've been asking everyone where you were and nobody cared to tell me!

Ant and Nasir both looked surprised at London, than each other. Ant's feeling were kind of hurt as it appeared she didn't even remember who he was. Sir not even knowing how to respond with a mouth full of cookies replied.

Hi! Umm how have you been?

London attempts to laugh and gets choked up a little. Both men scurry over to assist when London replies, I'm okay. Thank you! I knew one day you would get it right Sir. I'm not sure yet what happened but when I saw this ring on my finger. Both men looked at each other and flexed a look of confusion. Then Ant appeared to have a bright Idea. He wrinkled his forehead and nodded as to give Sir permission to claim the promise ring. Sir was a little slow at first but understood following Ant's lead.

Congratulations Sir! You didn't tell me you popped the big question!

Wwwwwell, ah I was trying to keep a low profile until she got better, you feel me? Sir not sure why Ant was doing this, but he didn't mind a bit. Ant low-key felt like a piece of shit, but selfishly felt why not take advantage of the situation and get out this way. Ant wanted to give his son a family and even though London was talking she still had a hell of a fight in front of her. Was what he did right? No, but for the time being Ant felt using Sir as his scape goat was perfect!

Knock, knock, knock! Bae! It's time to check out. The nurse needs you come on. Oh hi London, Sky says while making sure to rub her stomach talking.

Hi, London replies. I hope you're not here to start any shit with me and Sir like you did last time. I'm absolutely not well enough to have to deal with you. I see you rubbing your stomach. Sir please tell me that she is not having another supposed to be your baby!

No bitch with yo sick ass, I'm not having a baby by your no good ass man Sir. Who I am having a baby by is MY MAN ANT, and don't forget that shit either!

Well congratulations, and please excuse yourself as you aren't welcome here! (london waves her hand with the ring in the air).

Bae aren't you forgetting something?

Ant looks at Sky knowing exactly where this is about to go! No! Come on Sky let's go!

Yes please take her out of here, and if you know like I know you might want to get a blood test! I'm sure she has a discount with

Maury! Hahahahaha! Jazz manages to say while following suit with London and waving bye.

Later on that night, one of the biggest parties next to the cook-out was being thrown. One of the hood's finest had touched down and was ready to make his debut. He stayed out of sight his first two weeks home, but that was just to give the people time to prepare. They weren't ready for a kings release, but tonight they surely would be.

"Ochie Wally Wally, Ochie Bang Bang, Ochie Wally Wally, Ochie Bang Bang" Blast loud as hell in the club! It's hot, foggy and neon lights everywhere. DJ Handz is on with DJ Iceberg spinning. It's been a long time since the club was this lit! Nasir was home, Ant had just been discharged from the hospital and Nasir's right hand man Tony finally touched down from a three and a half year bid! The club was turnt and everyone knew tonight was going to be a good night!

Hey Tony! ladies would say as they walked by switching, almost popping blood vessels to get Tony's attention. Tony's older brother Lo was a G. He was real quiet and didn't pay much attention to drama. He was the out-of-sight type but would step up and handle his business if needed. Lo made sure when Tony touched down he wasn't missing a beat. The man had a fresh cut, "Tru Relegion" everything, with a crisp pair of construction "Timberland" boots. His smell was official "Issey Miyake". A large chain swung around his neck with custom Gold uppers he had molded just before he caught his case.

Ant and Nasir caught eye contact, which lead Ant to step to Sir. Look! I know what happened the other day was crazy but needed.

Listen I might be making a huge mistake but at the same time you could be too. Don't and I repeat don't hurt her. If you don't want to be with her get out of this now. London doesn't need any more stress on her than what she already has. I know things right now are a little foggy, but when reality set's back in are you going to ready for it and to face it?

First of all I didn't ask you to put me in the middle of that shit! Secondly I don't know if I want to be involved with that. I mean she's loss hella weight. Her hair is all gone, and the reality of her successfully beating this is indecisive, feel me! Like you got me caught up in the middle of some shit that I myself am unsure about!

Well she doesn't even remember me so I guess I am safe. Hahahaha. Who would have thought after everything we been through we would be having a conversation as such? We done damn near killed each other, went to jail because of each other, damn near killed each other again, and now we both looking stupid.

You looking stupid. The streets know who proposed to London so I'm good. I'm sure she is going to get her memory back. Well at least I pray she does. Meantime ama go back over here and celebrate with my man.

Okay! Tell a nigga I said welcome home. I'll send him over a bottle of "Ace of Spades" on me. The hood missed him. We need more througho niggas around. Tell him when he ready to get his feet wet, hit me up?

Oh and speaking of that, I need some work myself!

Hahahaha! I forgive you, but I don't forget my nigga!

The mood in the club changed. "Bryson Tyler" bangs loudly from the speakers. "Baby it's been that way! Baby it's been that way! Baby I still feel the same. Something I gotta maintain!

Suddenly Tashawna walks by Nasir slowly and very seductive. Switching while wearing a pink and nude sheer dress. Her smell was sweet, something unique. It was a mixed blend of flowers and fruit.

Damn ma! I know you not just going to walk by me that way, and not even speak! Nasir looks at her as if an angle just walked in the room. his eyes instantly became glossy, while his heart skipped a beat.

Damn nigga! You did leave me for dead. No call, no text, no nothing and you want me to say hi. Okay here goes. FUCK YOU! (Tashawna walks away giving Sir her middle finger.)

Wait! (Sir grabs her by her arm almost ripping her dress)

Wait what! Why? Aren't you getting married to that cancer having bitch in the hospital?

Chill B! Like that shit right there not even cool. That girl can't defend herself right now so why you coming for her like that? I was only complimenting you, but with that disrespectful shit you talking, bitch go that way! (Sir points in the direction of the door to the club).

I go in the direction I please with your weak ass! I knew you was fucking with that bitch!

Yeah! Well I knew you was jealous as hell and still are. You miss me, cool! You wanna fuck? Just say so. All that trying to be tough shit is not working. Like bitch you clowning yourself! You can front all you want for your fans, but that shit don't impress me.

Tashawna gets turned on by how calm Sir talks to her. Even though he was just defending ole girl London, she appreciated the respect he had and how he was checking her. She knew deep down she missed him and instantly started to wonder if what she had did in the meantime to make Sir jealous was about to push him away permanently.

Yo Tashawna! Hey baby what's good with you. (Toni walks over and smacks her on the ass)

Hey! (Not sounding too confident) What's up?

Fuck you mean what's up? Didn't I see you in the mall earlier buying the exact dress you got on now. We was kicking it, exchanged numbers, and decided to meet up tonight here. What you got amnesia or sumthin ma?

Bra! Hahahaha! This one of my shorties right here. Oh so you was mad thinking you was gone get somewhere kicking it with my nigga fresh home huh? This nigga right here my left. All he was gone do was fuck you and leave you be. This nigga fresh out of the penitentiary!

Pick ya head up ma, it's gone be okay! Tony cracks a smile and walks away to another shorty.

Damn! I'm so embarrassed. I guess I didn't do too good trying to make you mad huh?

NOPE

Sir steps in and grabs Tashawna around her waist. He looks her deep into her eyes and begins to kiss her lips. The kiss starts off as a peck only to lead into a wet sloppy and erotic exchange of tongues.

Let's go!

Okay!

************2 months later!************

Congratulations London! You have successfully accomplished phase one of your Chemo treatments, and with outstanding results. The Cancerous mass has decreased significantly. We here at Dr. Bauers appreciate your efforts to fight and will to trust us with your care. On your way out stop by the registration desk to sign off on the completion of phase one. Nurse Judy should have your schedule for phase two. Have some fun, but not too much fun. Relax and enjoy you are doing very well.

Thank you so much. My family and I do honestly appreciate everything you are doing for me. (London walks over and gives both nurses a huge hug and walks out to meet her mom in the car).

So your looking bright! Happy everything is looking good? I called Kia for you so you can go and get your hair done. If you feel up to it we can stop by the mall and grab a couple of things for you. We haven't been able to do much these last six months.

Right mom, we haven't. I'm a little tired, but we can still go. Maybe not do so much shopping as you know how after chemo my body needs a good rest.

Okay then. We can do just that. Both London and her mom shopped at "Macys", "H&M", "PINK", and "Buckle". London got more than she wanted or needed. While falling asleep in the car her mom looks over at her and tears watching her baby fighting ever so gracefully.

Wake up London your here. London your here. Come on baby. Kia is waiting. Your cousin Tiffany from Maryland sent you what she calls bundles of hair. Here take these and get done whatever you like. Your dad put an envelope in there and whatever is in it is yours. Kia has been paid already. If you need me to pick you up after just give me a call. I'm not going to BINGO until later on.

Okay mom and thank you. I'll call you if I need you.

Hey girl! (Kia, London's hairdresser waves excited to see her long-time friend and client) How you doing girl? I'm so glad you came in today to. Your mom told me all the good news when she made your appointment earlier. I'm so happy for you girl. Tonight they are having a little jam session at Buffalo Live. Your mom already okayed it if you wanna hang out, listen to some good music, eat some wings, and toss back a glass of wine or two! Hahahaha!

No wonder she took me to the mall. My mom's crazy. Sure I'll go. I just need to take my supplements and get some rest though.

Great! I made you a pre-braided cap. This way I can sew on the bundles. You'll be able to keep the hair longer and I can wash it for you to. An hour and half later, Kia says, Look girl! Dum, dum, dum. This hair is everything on you. You like it?

London turns around. Oh my God, yes! (tears begin to roll down London's face.) I look so beautiful. How can I thank you?

Girl don't get us all in here crying with you. We've been crying enough. You can make me happy by getting your stuff together and letting me drop you off to take a nap while I run to the beauty supply store. This way you will be ready when I come pick you up.

Okay sure, and thank you! Let me just call my mom.

Meanwhile as they pull up in front of London's home, both girls notice a unfamiliar car parked in the front of her home.

Girl do you know who that is?

No but something is telling me I do, or that I'm about to find out.

Okay girl I'll see you in a few. Call me if you need me.

Hello may I help you? Who are you looking for here?

Hi! My name is Caprisha are you London?

Yes! How may I help you?

The women reaches in her back seat and pulls out a box. After handing it to London she says: You've been served! Hahahahaha!

Served what, London speaks loudly to the woman as the woman get's in her car to leave. Oh well! I'll open it when I get in the house. I hope it's not anything to cause me harm. Maybe I should call my mom to come over and look at it with me. Nah! I'll wait. I need to take a quick nap so I can shower and get dressed. Geesh, I haven't been out in a long time. I wonder if I should go. Nasir may get mad if I do, but who care's anyways. Plus I haven't seen him in a week or so anyhow.

Ring, ring, ring!

Hello!

Did you open your box bitch? Click!

What? This is crazy? What the fuck is going on here? "London attempts to go get the box and open it, but instantly becomes distracted by what she sees on her couch.

WOW! This is so freaking beautiful! I love Pink, but this Royal Blue is saying something. Who would ever have brought me such an outfit as beautiful as this. It had to be mom!

Knock, knock, knock!

I see I am very popular today. Whoever could it be? Hello! Who is it?

Hey pretty, it's me!

It's me who? And how did you know whoever you are I was home?

It's your kids father silly and your mom told us you were home now open the door.

MOMMY! MOMMY! We're so glad our home. Me and Siyion love granny but we wanted so badly to come back home.

Yeah mom we did miss you. What was really wrong? Granny just kept telling us to pray and trust me we were.

Aww well first give me a kiss! MUAH! And second hug me so tight that we never part again.

Pinky swear mommy?

London sees Siyion wiping his eyes as he cries tears of joy, being able to see his mom and finally come home. This was everything to him and he wanted it to last.

You need anything from me cutie before I go? I just wanted to see you and bring the kids home. Your strong and amazing. Not to mention beautiful. I will always love you and that's a fact!

Chapter Eight

" All Darkness Has A Light"

Hey Sincere! Hey Siyion! How's auntie Nye's favorites?

We're good!

Okay then. Hop your butts in the bed. Mommy is going to go out for a little while and I'm going to stay here with you two. Hey what's in this box?

Hey girl thanks for coming over. Mommy really needed a break. As tired as I am, I can assure you, I won't be out long my damn self. I'm just happy to be out of the hospital myself. That box though, I honestly couldn't tell you. Some girl was parked in front of the house when Kia brought me home and she claim I was served. Then I received a phone call asking me if I had opened the box yet as well. The girl on the other end was rather nasty. I was going to wait and open it with mommy, but since you're here,

Since I'm here hell yeah we're going to open it. I don't know who these bitches think they are, but I tell you this. If any of the contents enclosed are a problem. I'm going to beat the shit out of every single person involved from the delivery person to the phone call person.

Nye you crazy. No wonder I love you so much.

Girl it's the truth. (Nye begins to cry) I thought I was going to lose my best..friend!

Awww girl don't get me started. I may look strong right now, but I'm still fighting. My emotions are a big part of my battle as well. Learning how to manage and control them is a big deal little do people know at this time.

I'm sure, hell I'm trying to manage my own as we speak. Well let's open this damn box, and see what all the uproar is about.

Both ladies walk into the kitchen and open the box over the sink. Out pours pictures! The pictures were those of Nasir with different women and Ant. What was worse was the letter attached.

Dear London,

Don't pride yourself thinking you're the better bitch because you're not! I know everything that I need to about you to get ahead again. Sadly everybody knows about you. As you look through the pictures you will find a sim-card attached to the back of one. Put it in your phone.

I'm sure you will be shocked at what you see but that's what your ass gets. Nasir is dumber than the average nigga. He isn't even aware that his sim-card is missing. If these pictures aren't enough I'm sure the graphic video recordings will hurt you even more. You see being Ms. Perfect gets you know where. There's even a video or two of you. I just thought your little sick ass might want to know how much either of your loves care about you especially Sir. Oh and heard you'd be out tonight! Brace yaself!

What the?

London you don't even need to go out tonight without me, I swear. If anything and I do mean anything should happen you call me. Seriously.

I'm good. Matter of fact I'm going to give him the sim card and letter tonight when I surprise him. It's a shame bitches can't leave me alone. I mind my business and like always they come for me. God is giving me a second chance at life. I'm not about to let this set me back, distract me or stress me at all.

Well alright then. If anything happens just call me!

Beep! Beep! Beep!

Okay Nye, that must be Kia. Sincere is knocked out and Siyion is in his room playing his play station 4. I promise you I won't be out long and will call you if I need you. Muah! London kisses Nye on her cheek and hugs her tight before she walks out of the door.

Hey girl you look cute! I like the way that blue is looking on you girl.

You do? Geesh I haven't been out in so long that I wasn't sure if I put myself together right. London was wearing a form fitting royal blue dress from "BEBE". It had an open back with a tight strap above her rear. The front was just as dynamic. It dipped straight down the front allowing cleavage to be seen, but just enough to leave a sexy impression. The dip cut right above her belly button with a steep split on the right leg. Although the dress was thigh length the split was cut just enough to expose her flower printed tattoo.

The shoes she wore were yellow, and with a matching bag from "Aldo". Her scent was of a soft linen smell. Kind of like fresh laundry. Nye was a cold make-up artist and made sure her best friend was ready to kill on sight! London had no idea what was about to take place but she was definitely going to be the reason.

Okay girl you ready?

Yes Ma'am!

I knew it was going to lit tonight so I managed to get us VIP! You know I wouldn't have anything else for my girl especially after all you have been through!

Oh okay cool! Thanks love!

As the girls approach the VIP entrance, they have to walk by the regular admission line. While the club is blasting a classic through back by Usher "Confessions" both new and old heads were stunned by the appearance of London. It was almost as if they had seen a ghost!

Damn who's that?

Hey girl come here?

What's yo name baby?

Is that London?

I thought she was sick!

Don't she got Cancer?

God Damn she fine!

Ayeeeee! Girl you are so the talk of the night! I'm glad my girl came out. Look! There's Michelle and Andre over there. Come on. Let's get us a drink.

London was excited about all the talk she was causing, but she also was starting not to feel so good. Trying hard not to let it show she kindly asked for a cup of water with fresh cut lemon. While she sat up at the bar a very handsome man felt the need to approach.

Hello beautiful! Is your name London?

Why yes it is. If I may ask is your name Anthony?

Why yes it is.

They both start to laugh so hard as she thought it was super cute how he approached her.

Damn girl you look so damn good! How are you doing if you don't mind me asking?

Well I finally completed my last set of Chemo today. I have another part to take, but from what the doctors are telling me, everything is going well, and my lump has shrunken significantly.

Damn London that's good! Give me a hug. I'm so proud of you! They both engage in a hug so enduring that London and Ant almost kiss.

Wooo! That was crazy or am I crazy. You and Nasir ae still cool right?

Yes!

Than why did it feel like I had been in your arms before. I mean like that wasn't your normal hug there. The way we shared.

London! Hey girl what's up? Long time no see. You cute in all but uh. He's taken!

Okay. I mean I wasn't trying to take your man. From the looks of it he was trying to be taken. If he willing to be taken this easy then you my dear should get you a new one!

London chill! Hahahaha! She's not my girl. You know I'm still tryng to figure out shit with Sky and that's our son's god mother. Pay her no mind please. Stacey chill it's all good here.

Yeah okay! That little bitch need to watch her mouth!

Cough, cough, cough.

Chill Stacey, Shorty you okay?

Yes bae I'm fine, I mean Ant. I'm fine. I'll be right back.

Damn that girl still has my heart. Sky ass is due in three more months. Did I make a mistake or was this just how things were supposed to play out!

Yo brah! You still fucking with the girl that was in the hospital?

Nah why you ask that?

Cause she fine as hell. Can I hit that?

WHAT? Fuck you mean she fine as hell. Where you see London at?

Damn my bad fool. She just walked into the bathroom.

Nah my nigga she still in the hospital. I know you ain't seen her.

Well she has a twin then, cause I know what and who I saw.

And why do you care anyways Nasir? Tashawna interrupts checking Sir about his ex.

Man girl get the fuck out of my face. Don't you ever try and clown me in front of my niggas.

Yo there shorty go right there!

Damn! You was right!

Nasir stares at her as she walks out of the women's room. The way she appeared was almost as if to be an angle. The last time Sir saw London she looked as if she was damn near dead. Weighing about 120 pounds, completely bald headed, face sagging on both sides due to the excessive weight loss, and a hardly able to keep anything down.

If there were any words that he could manage to get out of his mouth, it was Damn! Instantly feelings became fresh. No one

appeared to matter anymore. All of a sudden he remembered the
ring Ant gave her, which was noticeably missing. Sir knew he
needed to address her, but he needed help with how.

Whew! I had to pee.

You alright? Just let me know whenever you're ready to leave. I
was worried about you.

All girl I'm okay. I want to dance come on. That's my song
playing. "Can't raise a man" "He got older but never grew" "For
his life he can't tell the truth" As London sings she sway's her hips
back and forth seductively. All of the team head to the floor and
stare. As all the ladies chimed in singing, London stood out the
most.

Nasir caught a glimpse of Ant across the room staring. The way he
looked at her mad Sir jealous. Tashawna was in the cut paying
Nasir much attention as well. She began to create an agenda as to
make her presence known, while reminding London that Nasir was
now her man.

As the song begins to dye down, what was coming on next was
going to do it. "When I pull back them sheets" "Girl you gone
think I invented sex". Ant just can't take it. He goes in. Walking up
behind her they rock to the beat instantly. The flow between the
two was like magic.

Something was all too familiar about the grace and touch this man
had on her, and she was eager to find out why this attraction was
so right. Her soul told her as he grabbed her waist and turned her

around. Looking in her eyes he inadvertently blurted out "I love you London and I always have".

What was said he had no idea of, but what was about to happen. Just continue to read.

Yo what the!

What the what my nigga. I think it's time we tell the truth.

The truth? Hahaha! Oh you want to look like the biggest loser I see huh? Cool let's go. Where would you like me to start first? How about telling her that the reason why she can't remember shit is due to the coma she was in. Oh and that beautiful diamond promise ring you was rocking. He bought it! He proposed to you until he found out Sky your friend was having his baby while you was looking dead as hell.

London!

Oh and I already wasn't fucking with you, but this great and amazing guy figured since you didn't remember him or shit yal had to put everything on me. You see I haven't been in contact with you. Hell I didn't even know you came home. Hahaha!

Sir that shit is not right. What you so mad for?

Kia get the fuck out my face yo! Tashawna smack this bitch!

I wish she would!

Tashawna? My cousin Tashawna?

Yeah your fake ass cousin. Don't tell me you forgot she was my girl too? Damn ma. I think you should take your sick ass home, before you get your feelings hurt.

London instantly gets a headache. Tears begin to roll down her pretty face. Why is it always me, being made a fool. What did I ever do to you, for you to hurt me so bad Sir?

You Fucked him! Bet you didn't remember that now did you! Weak dick ass nigga. Funny how you ain't remember shit about him, but you sure did remember my ass. Probably cause I put in that work! (Sir chants loudly while holding his dick laughing).

You are so fucking cruel. Couldn't be me! I would have smacked fire out of his ass by now. London dry your eyes. This nigga ain't shit! Let's go! His feelings just hurt you not all over his marshmallow ass!

Who in the fuck are you calling a marshmallow? You clowning huh? Bitch you just mad nobody wants your raggedy ass pussy.

Bae chill! We don't have time to be arguing with nobody. Especially her sick ass. Bitch shouldn't you be home with your kids. Better yet, what time is the nurse coming over? Don't you have cancer!

You think that shit funny Tashawna? Say that shit up close! I might be sick, but I'll still beat your ass.

You won't do shit! You better be careful. You might get readmitted. London tries to reach over the crowd and punch Tashawna but only grazes her jaw. Ant sees a side of London he never knew existed. Watching her inner gangster in full format made him scurry over.

Fuck him and I mean that! Ant grabs London's arm and pulls her into his chest. Listen just go straight home. I promise you I'll take care of this clown and his entourage. I love you man and I promise you I'll make this all right! As London goes to leave Tashawna manages to through her shoe and pop London in the back of her head.

I'll be back bitch and I promise that! Wait on it!

63

Chapter Nine

"Who Has The Gun Now"

As Kia drove London home she counseled her attempting to uplift her spirits. Girl fuck them. You are strong, beautiful, loving and ambitious. Any man who gets you should be honored to have you. You don't need any man who thinks less of you, puts you down, and doesn't want to see you grow! He is not for you. God will present and trust me you will know!

All while they ride London appears to be paying Kia attention; however, she is distracted by a repetitive voice. She keeps hearing it say "I need you to get better". "I'll be here every day until you do".

Hey girl you hear me! We here! London! London! LONDON!

Ooh! Sorry girl huh!

I said we here. You need me to come in with you?

No girl I'm okay, plus Nye is in the house. Thanks so much for the great time. I know that I need to be done with Nasir and after tonight, that's exactly what I plan on doing.

Good, cause honey. That mouth on Sir will have you in jail quick. He's very lucky I don't have a man, cause boy if I did. You and I probably wouldn't be friends.

Why you say that?

Cause any man that I deal with street or not will not be tolerating no clown ass, bum ass, disrespectful piece of shit!

I totally understand but girl thanks. I'll call you tomorrow okay?

Okay! Take care girl!

I will! London hops out the car and goes into the house. Hey Nye! I'm home. Thanks so much.

Girl your bed is comfortable as hell! Did you have fun?

Yes I sure did. (Lying as she didn't want to draw attention to her).

Okay girl, well the kids are both sleep. I'm going to stop over Vinny's and see what he's up too. I hope he's horny as I want some, feel me? Hahahahaha!

Girl you a fool. Text me and let me know you made it okay?

Okay! Love you girl and I'm glad you had fun.

Muah!

Muah!

Finally. Now I know that bitch didn't think hitting me with that shoe was going to fly. And her nigga! Oh okay. I guess he needs to really meet who the fuck I am! London takes off her outfit and pins up her hair. Black cargos and a black tee was all that was needed.

She bent down in the bathroom and said a quick prayer before zooming out of the house.

Lord I know that you ask better of me; however, you know that I am far from perfect. I am so tired of everyone doubting my strength and mistaking my kindness as a weakness. Lord please watch over my children as they lay here sleep and watch over me more. I know what I am about to do is wrong but it is needed.

Pulling up behind the train station London is able to view the entire crowd as they come out. All of a sudden she sees her target and pulls right up!

So bitch you was bad in the club what's up! Pow! London knocks the shit out of Tashawna to the point she hits the ground. While climbing on top of her she attempts to punch her continuously, until she is pulled up off of her by Nasir.

London what the fuck is wrong with you. Take your ass home. Slightly turned on as he had never seen her go to war, Tashawna felt she was snuck off guard. No sooner than London arrives home thinking everything was all over a car pulls up right behind her.

BITCH! You was just going to sneak me huh?

London thinks to herself (Did this bitch just pull up to my house) and then smiles as she knows exactly what's about to happen! Watching both Nasir and one of his friends get out of her car with her friends fueled the fire even more.

Running down her driveway prepared she yells Bitch you gone get what you looking for today! Pow! Straight hit in her mouth. Pow another to her left cheek with a swift combination of left rights and a upper cut to her ass.

Bitch you think pulling my wig off was supposed to lighten up this ass whipping? NOT! Instant head lock followed by a kick to Tashwana's nose.

London heard it pop and instantly became excited. Sad but it turned her on being able to beat her ass as bad as she was. Nasir's friend Sticks tried to break it up numerous times but each time she found some way to get in that ass. Finally it was over. Tashawna hopped in her car with her friends who by the way watched crying. Once she pulled off leaving behind Nasir and Sticks she gracefully picked her wig up and walked back in her house.

London! Bam! Bam! London! Let me in yo! We need to talk.

Brah. I don't think she wants to hear shit you have to say right about now.

Man fuck that! Did you see her though? She got straight in Tashawna ass. I swear I didn't think she had it in her.

That's what you get. On some real man to man shit you foul. That's a good woman right there. I been seen it but after tonight, I'm for certain. Like how many women you know can go through all she's been through and still come out strong. That's the kind of woman right there you protect, honor and cherish. Not even going to front, but every nigga been wishing they had that!

WHAT! You really think you can just tell me to my face am a loser huh? Damn! I really fucked up huh?

Yeah my nigga you sure did. From the looks of it you and ya man can leave! What you need a ride? Clown ass still walking around huh? Don't look so surprised. I told you I was coming for mines.

Ant you got balls I see.

And you still broke I see. That's a nigga like yours problem today.

You too busy being concerned with pussy when you should be getting money. Learn the difference between counterfeit and real too. Seems you manage your money the same way you manage your bitches! That's why you choose a counterfeit version of a real woman.

Fuck you Ant!

Two cars pull up with squad members for both Ant and Nasir. London comes running out of the house. Nasir why are you still here. Get the fuck away from here! I never want to see your no good for nothing but drama and STD's ass again.

Bitch! Sir attempts to raise his hand as if to smack London.

Nah! Slow ya row big pimping. Let her go! You wrong Sticks says. We all know that you are wrong. The team is not here to side with you, but to make sure you leave without being any more of a stress to this girl. London I am deeply sorry and I wish you well.

Ant do what you have to, to make this diamond shine as bright as she was tonight forever.

Real Nigga Shit! Thanks

Sir puts his head down and hops in the car with Sticks and his crew. Knowing deep he really fucked up he wasn't really ready to believe it, but out of respect walked away.

Hey baby you okay? What the fuck happened? I told you to come straight home and wait on me. Instead I received about 6 missed calls and hella text messages telling me you was whopping Tashawna ass. Hahahaha! It's not funny but damn bae, you don't even look like you did that.

Well she shouldn't have thrown that shoe at me!

I can't believe this shit! (Tashawna crying & driving) I can't believe he just let her sneak me three times. How the fuck did she just get that opportunity three fucking times.

Listen girl. You one don't need to be crying over no nigga that really has no care for you, and two didn't even try to stop the fight.

You would know wouldn't you as you didn't try and help me either.

Excuse me! Look you got your ass beat and that's it! She never snuck you, not even once since I seen everything. You picked on the right one. If you mad you mad. You should be mad at that low life nigga you probably still going to fuck with when we get out. Matter of fact you can pull over. We good ma! Real friends respect real shit. You mad at your own wrong doings. That beef had nothing to do with you, but you wanted to flex trying to impress and got your ass beat!

Get out! Get the fuck out my shit!

Ya mama's shit bitch and we will! Let's go Toya! (Both ladies hop out and walk into the nearest store to await a ride).

Ooooooooooh! I can't believe how this shit happened tonight. My fucking face bleeding, this bitch done snuck me and this nigga.

Bzzzzzz, Bzzzzzz, Bzzzzzz.

Text#1: Hey baby I'm sorry. Come pick me up

Text #2: I know you mad please come get me

Text #2 reply: FUCK YOU!

Text #3: I love you I swear I really do

London I have to be honest with you. I fucked up. When you were in the hospital I did put that promise ring on your finger. I told you how I needed you to get better for me so we could be together, and that I was going to visit you every day until then. I meant it so I thought until I found out Sky was having my first son. She was standing there looking so good, I must admit I wasn't sure if you were going to pull through, so I made a decision and choose her.

Well! At least now I know who said that to me. For the entire day I have been hearing that same sentence repeatedly playing in my head. Now to find out that you were the culprit. So tell me this? Was Nasir right saying I fucked you?

Yes!

Than to me that makes you no better than him. You left me when I needed you the most. Like why would you do that to someone you say you love. Love just isn't something you play with.

I know bae! You have no idea how I felt. In all honesty I haven't been really happy since I walked away. Can I make it right with you please? Can I?

I honestly don't know. After what I've been through I think I need a break. Call me in a day or so. I'm pooped. As she went to walk away Ant grabbed onto her and planted a kiss that even made his knees weak.

London I can't be without you and I promise you I won't. Whatever I need to do I will. Watch me. I promise.

BZZZZZZ. BZZZZZZ. BZZZZZZZ.

Text #1: Ant 911 get to the hospital quick

Text #2: Sky's in labor and it's not good!

Why would you want me to pick you up?

You came didn't you!

How you just gon let that girl sneak me three times?

I didn't let her sneak shit! To be honest you jumped in some shit that you shouldn't of. Nobody told you to throw your shoe at her and think that shit was funny. I'm a grown ass man who didn't need your help. Now we can either argue all night or we can go to your house.

Let's go! You talking about you want to go to my house huh? Yeah well let me do you the honor and drop you off where you need to be. Tashawna pulls up in front of London's house yelling for Sir to get out. As soon as London sees what's going on she scurries out on her porch.

Oh did you leave something? What I know you two didn't come back to have that ass beat again? Suddenly the car pulls off and London goes back inside. I'm not about to play with them. Especially tonight.

You really a stupid ass bitch for doing that. I should have let her beat your ass again. For real! Matter of fact let me out. I'm good. I'll catch a ride from one of the homies. I'm starting to think how I really fucked up.

That's right! You sure did. Get out of my shit and lose my fucking number. You a weak dick nigga anyways, who's only good for eating pussy and licking my ass.

Aww you big mad you got that ass beat aren't

POW! POW! POW!

What's wrong? Where she at?

Labor and delivery room 316. Hurry up their waiting on you!

Push! 1-2-3-4

Push! 1-2-3-4

Push! Wait! CODE BLUE! I repeat CODE BLUE!

Hand me the scissors. He's turning blue! Somehow he managed to get wrapped in-between the umbilical cord. Get the support units here fast!

What's going on in there? Man I don't hear my son and it's way too many people in that room!

Okay. He's a little fighter. Come on little guy! Where's that support unit? I need it fast!

Beeeeeeeeeeeeeeeeeeeeeep!

We lost the little guy.

Noooooooooo! Nooooooooo! Not my boy! Not my baby! Not my boy! Doctors please save him. Try again! Please save him!

Ma'am we are very sorry. It appears that he was tangled severely with your umbilical cord. He was already in cardiac arrest which is what caused an early pregnancy. Would you like to hold him?

OH MY GOD! NOOOOOOOOO! MY BABY! NOOOOOOOO!

Ant hears Sky crying and attempts to storm in the room, but is stopped by Sky's father and brothers.

The Doctor comes out and asks: Is the Father here?

Yes! I'm here Doctor. What's wrong? Is my son okay? Can I see him? Why isn't he crying?

Sir sincerely with my deepest regards and condolences. He didn't make it. We tried all that we could; however, the little guy was strangled by the umbilical cord and went into cardiac arrest. We are allowing the parents a moment with the body before they take him away. Would you like to come in?

And that's just it huh? He didn't make it come see him. Mannnn. Why didn't you let me in when I tried. Why did all of you keep me away from seeing my little man at least try and fight! He was/is a fighter! I know it in my heart. I can felt him.

DOCTOR! DOCTOR! QUICK! THE BABY!

All of a sudden there was a faint almost like a whisper cry. Baby Ant was a fighter and was trying to fight even more. The Doctor quickly hurried in with Ant sure to follow. Baby Ant was rushed in the incubator to the ICU unit for preemies. Ant knew his mother heard his prayer and fell to his knees with tears in his eye's holding Sky's hand praying even harder.

************ Early Morning News ************

Last night shots were fired on the intersection of Main an Fillmore Avenue. One man pronounced dead on the scene, a young woman shot two times in the head in critical condition, another young man shot once in the head and the second in his back also in critical condition, while another young man was grazed on his left shoulder. Each of the victims were rushed to ECMC. No charges have been filed as the shooter is still on the loose.

Damn how did I miss that. I must was tired as hell. Shit that's right up the street from me. Well prayers to the life lost and the one's fighting for their life as we awaken unbothered. Whew! I swear I never want to experience that again. Words couldn't explain my thoughts and feelings while I just laid there almost non-existent to the world. The worse part was awakening and not being able to put all the pieces of the puzzles together.

Ring. Ring. Ring.

Hello!

London baby how are you?

I'm okay. May I ask who I am speaking with?

Yes baby it's Nasir's mom Ms. Luretha.

Yes! Yes! Yes! Hello mom how are you? I am so sorry I didn't recognize the voice. I'm sure you are already aware that some of my memory has been impaired, but only temporarily.

Yes baby I know. Nasir did make mention to me that much before.

Before?

Before he was shot midmorning on Main and Fillmore.

Oh no! Can't be? London starts to rethink last night's events, and how she had just saw them pull back up in front of her house before she went in and fell asleep. Is he okay? (London's voice starting to shake while talking).

Well baby he's fighting. Crazy part is all he's asking for is you. He is unconscious, but every once in a while he mumbles London!

Bzzzzzz. Bzzzzzz. Bzzzzzzz.

London reads her text messages while still on the phone with Ms. Luretha.

Text #1: OMG Baby last night was crazy. I almost lost my son but he's here.

Text #2: He's very small, 3 pounds 12 oz and fighting like hell. I named him Champion Anthony Jackson!

Text #3: I'll be at the hospital until they tell me he's good, but in the meanwhile I just wanted you to know I love you!

Text #3 Reply: I'm so happy for you. I will pray for you and your bundle of joy. Take your time and focus on him.

Text#4: I will and thank you!

London. London. London.

Yes I'm here!

Well I don't know if I'm asking too much of you and I most certainly understand if I am, but would you mind coming to the hospital later on?

Beep!

Hold on please. (London clicks her line)

Baby!

Yes mom.

Tashawna was killed last night!

Chapter Ten

"Predictions"

*********** One Week Later ************

Well it is what it is. I feel bad in all she was murdered, but I personally didn't know her and from the looks of it, she was plotting on London not making it her damn self. Care? Not!

Jazz you jive have a point right there. It's like all the bitch was concerned about was Nasir. Family or not once she found out what was up, she should have just walked away.

That's how I feel too Nye, like really. One minute you claimed to be the cousin and would never mess with no nigga that clown like that, but was working hard trying to compete. I'm glad London beat the brakes off her grimey ass. It's a fucked up thing to say I know, but I'm even glad my brother got shot too!

Yeah he needed that slow down. London is really an amazing woman. She attended Tashawna's funeral. Laid a pretty bed of flowers on her casket, while managing to come here every single day not spazzing out!

Right! It takes a special kind of lady to be able to do all of that and still smile. I heard the baby is doing well too. It will still be sometime before he can come home but he is fine. That girl Sky had the baby at the hospital I work at so it's easy to check on the updates. Ant is a real good man too. He spends all his time there. His face all fuzzy. Hell from the looks of him, one would say he lost a couple pounds too.

Damn!

Lord! As you have blessed me with the opportunity to awaken, and live life more fulfilling then before. I would like to ask you do provide this man with the same opportunity. Please open his mind and heart to understand love and happiness. As he is scorned, he is in need of guidance from someone stronger than me. As he is an unfaithful servant of you, touch down on his spirit so that he may get to know the power of you. Lord I pray this prayer because it is custom too his needs. Unlike him, I will be here until you tell me not to. Unlike him, I will take care and manage his needs accordingly. Continue to give me the strength needed and that is all I will ask.

After saying her prayers, London grabs a basin, soap, towels and new bedding. She made sure as a part of her daily routine, Nasir slept/rested comfortably and clean. He was unable to eat as he went in and out of consciousness often. A feeding tube was supplied to keep him full. He stopped trying to mumble her name as he saw her every day. As a way of expressing himself he would blink his eyes hard and ball up his fist. When London would see this she kindly kissed his forehead and stuck her pinky finger in his fist to hold.

Hey baby. Mama's here. Although London prayed daily Nasir still had selfish ways. Hearing his mom come in, most times he would close his eyes or simply turn his head as far as it could go. I know you hear me boy! I tell you this, and you can blink to let me know you understand me. This young lady is by far the most beautiful soul you could ever meet. I hope you are aware of everything she has sacrificed for you. This girl is heaven sent!

Sir starts batting his eye's uncontrollably to the point where they realize he's having a seizure.

HELP!

Sky you are an amazing woman. I am very proud to have you in my life as my son's mother. Champ is the greatest thing ever, to happen to me.

Hmmm your son's mother? So now I'm just your son's mother. Wow!

Sky listen. You and I both know that my heart has always been with London. Having Champ is wonderful and I have no regrets, but my heart isn't complete with you and I'd be a sucka ass nigga if just fucked with you because I could. Your beautiful so don't settle for that.

A tear begins to roll down Sky's face. So where do we go from here?

Well for starters let's agree to be awesome parents. No interference with significant others unless they are problematic to our child. Play with me if you want too. Let's maintain our friendship and respect for one another. Neither one of us try to manipulate our power or use our child against each other. I'm not a child support nigga, I'm a man who does more than support his. You get what I'm saying. I want him every other week like I get my daughter. Matter of fact the same week I have her. This way they will know each other, and form a brother sister bond. Let's be respectful of each-others request, limitations, and space please.

Okay! I can't say that I am totally happy with this, but I respect your decision, and way of handling everything. Now I'll be honest. I don't know how to feel about you having my baby around London right away, but I'll pray on it. There is still time before he will be able to come home anyhow and my request is that when the doctors feel it's a good idea to bounce him back and forth, then I will oblige.

Then I guess we're getting off to a good start!

Who may I ask is the health care proxy for the patient named Nasir?

Umm, That would be me. I'm his mother.

Due to the severe loss of blood, in order to improve the patients chances of recovery we suggest him having a blood transfusion. After being shot in the lower cerebellum, I would highly suggest it.

Okay yes doctor.

What we will need to do first is test him for HIV, Aids and other communicable infections. Should any of these be present we may have to improvise a different strategy for improvement. If you agree to all the information I have just discussed with you, please sign your name where the yellow stickers are located. Once you are done, I will place a RUSH stamp to have this processed immediately. In the meantime if you complete as much as you know about the patients past history.

Yes Doctor I will. London. Hahahaha. I think you might be a little better with filling this out rather me.

Okay mom sure. London reads over the background request and says: Sexual Contac History in the last 6 months! Well mom, I'm not sure I can answer this one completely correctly. Hahahaha

When Nasir comes back he is speaking but with a severe slur. He calls out to London and with tears streaming down his face he attempts to say I love you. Watching his struggle was painful as all she could do was keep her head up and fight back tears of love and pain. She knew all too well what that feeling was like; however, she wasn't going to run. Her model was always "Two wrong don't make a right" an she tried hard to live by that.

Ring. Ring. Ring.

Hello!

Hey my love, how are you?

I'm fine, may I ask who I'm speaking with?

Damn shorty you forgot my voice already? I know it's been a rough 3 weeks, but uh I haven't forgotten about you. What's good it's Ant!

Oh okay hello!

Oh okay hello. Did I catch you at a bad time or something?

No uh not really. I was just at the hospital with Nasir.

Damn okay that is right. I was so caught up with making sure my little champ was alright I forgot to inquire about him getting shot. I'm also sorry for your loss. Despite what went on between you and your cousin I'm sure her losing her life was difficult.

Honestly it wasn't. I prayed and left my words with her and the Lord. Nasir is doing. Things are not perfect but he's doing. At this time he is still unable to walk.

Damn I know how that feels!

Right now he as a language barrier. His speech is was significantly impacted by the gunshot wound to his lower cerebellum. He blinks when he can't get words out and balls up his fist.

Okay. Well call me later. I have something to tell you but in person only!

************ 9 pm ****************

Awwww why thank you! Ant arrives with his signature gift for London. Three dozen roses. One pink, one yellow and one white.

You knew I wasn't going to come empty handed. Hey where are the kids?

Oh Sincere is over Nye's as she is getting her hair braided and Siyion is with my mom. He has football practice in the morning and my father lives to side-line coach! Hahahaha.

That's cool. Well of course I wasn't just going to bring you something and not the kids. This is the doll house I promised Sincere while you were in the hospital and all the dolls and furniture she picked out. Siyion has the Play Station 5 limited edition with 300 games already downloaded for him. I didn't want them to think with so much going on I forgot about them. Ant puts his head down feeling ashamed. I really didn't mean to hurt you or the kids and especially our mother.

I understand. How's Sky and Champ doing?

Well Champ is fighting and it's looking good. I'm so prayerful for my little man it's crazy. Sky well. That's what I wanted or should I say needed to talk to you about.

Okay?

I told her I love you!

Ant! Why would you do this at a time like this. Your baby is fighting needing both of his parents and I have obligated myself to be there for Nasir at a time when he has no one barely.

My timing may have been bad but it needed to be done. I figured she understand that now so that we could be supports for each other without any ill feelings. I'm going to always be there for her just as you are doing for Nasir despite all that you two have gone through.

Now, now my friend! Let us not go there. At least he bought me a cheap ass $100 ring and had every intention of making sure everyone knew. You promised me in the midst of me possibly dying and then chose to leave me for dead and use him as your scape goat. How dare you pass judgement, but you love me. Right! Sir was by far not the best, but I always knew what to expect. You on the other hand wowed me away with your kind words, quality time, and immaculate love making skills only to leave me when I needed you the most! Oh my God! Did you just hear that?

Hear what?

Everything I just said!

Duh, how could I not!

No stupid. I'm starting to remember things. I remember you in the hospital doing that. I can recall hearing your every word while I felt your every touch. I just was unable to open my eyes and speak my feelings to you.

Damn. Okay! Well what else do you remember?

I don't know. I mean you just tool me to a place where it enabled partial memory and now I can express it.

Well how about. Right then and there Ant kisses London as passionately as he could. She didn't resist or deny him either.

While standing the kitchen Ant manages to pick her up and place her on top of her counter top. Still exchanging saliva they both manage to reconnect. London tells Ant how she felt when he left her, and how hurt she was being unable to express it. I'm sorry baby I really am and I promise you from this day forward I will never leave you again. Tomorrow I have something planned that I would like to share with you.

What about Champ. Don't you have to go to the hospital tomorrow, and I myself have to make sure Sir is washed and prepared for the day.

No you don't! I've already spoken to his mother and she has you covered. Sky is also ware and told me it was okay to take a day off. I also brought you something to wear tomorrow with the help of Nye and Sincere.

Oh really?

Yes really. I don't want to spoil what I have planned so before this night goes any farther I am going to leave. Open this envelope tomorrow as soon as you awake. There's specific instructions on how tomorrow will go from start to finish.

Hmmm.

Hmmm what? Just know that I am a man of my word and you have taught me more than anything how to stay that way. I don't know if everything that is about to happen could happen without everyone who has been involved involvement. This was difficult but needed. Just know that I love you and I hope that your satisfied with my attempts to be a better man tomorrow.

Well we will just have to see about this. I do know who I will be calling as soon as you walk out that door and that's a fact. Nye and Sincere sneaky asses. Hahahahahaha

Ms. Lureatha!

Yes Doctor!

If we could take the time to discuss the what we have come to develop in Nasir's recovery plan. At this time he has made a significant improvement speech wise as we believe the lack there of, of proper blood flow was restricting his ability to speak and pronounce words properly. This is only temporary and a successful recovery we aspire to have. He will be wheel chair bound but with continuous rehab therapy walking will again be possible. He has lost function of some organs that I am not sure he will be able to understand. Erections may be difficult.

My dear!

Yes he will be able to use it just not as frequent as he may wish. His jaw will only allow his mouth to open minimally, so when he does speak it may sound a little slurish but he will manage. His left hand will not open to its full extent, causing his hand to look deformed. He can wear a special glove to keep his fingers spread out; however, he will not be able to close it while wearing the glove. The glove is only used to assist with providing a normal appearance not performance or function.

God is good and that it all I can say. I could very well have been burying my son and God did not see fit for that to be. With all this being said I will continue to pray as always God has the final word.

True! Well I just wanted to step in before discharge orders were final. He should be looking to go home in a day or so. I also understand that he received emergency Medicaid as he did not have active insurance on arrival. He does not qualify for a variety of programs to assist with assistive devices, but someone who wishes to remain anonymous donated very device suggested.

Rise and Shine it's 9 am! Rise and Shine it's 9 am! London's alarm clock went off like crazy. Today was a big morning. Due to the allergic reaction she had during her Chemo phase one a more enhanced and expensive form of Chemo was no being used.

Ding Dong! Ding Dong! Knock, knock. Knock.

Hello!

Good morning beautiful it's nurse Kim. I'm here for your Chemo are you ready?

Yes, yes! Why sure. If you would just set up here and allow me to run and brush my teeth I'll be right out.

Okay no problem. I'll just begin setting up. By the way did you eat?

Uh no. I apologize.

Okay no worries just get yourself together.

As London walks out of the bathroom she sees placed beautifully on her dining room table a petite breakfast. It included toast, scrambled eggs with cheese, grapes, peaches, mangos, and

pineapples with a strawberry banana smoothie. Wow! How did?
Who?

Okay Dear. As I prepare your treatment and I.V.'s you just sit
pretty and eat. Oh and someone told me to remind you to read the
instructions for today.

Oh my God! Not you too. Hmmm. How he has even managed to
get my nurse in on the swing of things is nuts. London smiled big
and bright. Before she knew it, her second series treatment number
one was done.

Ring. Ring. Ring.

Hello!

Hey girl, what's up?

Nothing much. Just finished treatment number one of my last part
of Chemo.

Okay! How did you do?

Oh everything went well.

Great. So what are your plans for today?

Honestly I don't know. Ant wrote out an intense letter planning out
my entire day. Hell he even managed to get my nurse involved. I
questioned why when she arrived it was thirty minutes earlier then
the previously scheduled time, but since she had to sneak the
breakfast in.

Awwww! How was the breakfast?

It was good!

Okay well did you shower and get dressed yet?

No! I actually just sat down for a minute. I wanted to drink a cup of coffee and relax seeing as this is the first time in three weeks I haven't had to go to the hospital and take care of Nasir.

Right. Well open the door.

Open the door?

Yup! Open the door.

Surprise!

Surprise what?

Welp I guess you should have read the letter. Angie and myself are here to assist you with getting your day started. First we will make sure you take the bath of your life, while getting your outfit for right now together. When you hop out of the tub, Angie will be giving you a full body massage. Alisha should be on her way in an hour as she will be supplying you with a full facial and light beat. Me of course will get that hair of yours in order!

Yo have to be kidding me.

Nope!

This can't really be happening.

Awww girl you so deserve it! Don't get me over here crying and shit as I just put these lashes on. Plus Andre' already mad that I'm not coming in till later.

Okay, well I guess I'll get ready.

Ding Dong!

Okay wait! Now who could this be? You said Alisha wasn't coming until an hour or so.

I honestly don't know. Your guess is good as mines here.

London walks over to the door and says: Who is it?

UPS!

UPS?

When London opens the door she is overwhelmed by the size of the box standing in front of her, as it's taller than her. The UPS man asks where would you like this to go?

Umm, you can put it over there. By the fire place actually.

Okay and sign here please. Thank you!

As soon as the UPS man leaves the girls hurry over to open up the box. Once the box was opened there was of course Ant's signature delivery. Three dozen roses colored yellow, white and pink, with a huge Teddy bear. The best part of the gift was yet another out fit with a matching bag and sneakers, and a little teacup Yorkie. The dog's name was Cupid. She was absolutely beautiful. Her pink bow a-top of her head was the cutest. The instructions read to make sure she attended each of today's events and was dressed accordingly as well. The girls all ooh and ahhed over the cute puppy clothing Cupid had.

Finally London was ready and in great timing.

Knock, knock, knock! Hey baby you ready?

When she came down the stairs she looked amazing. The sundress she wore was not only a perfect fit, but a perfect match for her beauty. It accented every one of her facial features making her more beautiful each time Ant stared at her.

Part one of his date consisted with him taking London on a Canal side boat ride. Here he was able to pour into her soul by just being real and showing her the man he awaited to be. They talked of everything they could imagine. From favorite colors and food, to likes and dislikes. It was the perfect way to go into lunch.

We have to go to the house, so we can get ready for lunch!

Ant knew to prepare his belongings so he packed his travel bags. As they hopped out of the car with Cupid fast asleep they went into the house to prepare for lunch.

I don't know how to say thank you. I've honestly felt so amazing today, that there are no words I could use.

Well don't worry about words. Actions speak louder. I told you I was going to show you what I meant didn't I?

Yes you did. As perfect as today is going Ant I honestly am not ready to put myself back into something that could hurt me or cause hurt to me.

Babe girl listen. The day is not over so don't say anything else yet. I'm not done showing you the man I can well will be. There will be a specific time during dinner when you can tell me and whatever happens, happens. I'm prepared either way.

Hump! You don't have to say it like that either.

Shut-up spoiled and give me a kiss.

They engage in a quick heart felt kiss with a quick pop on London's ass. Come on girl get ready we have plan's my love we have plan's.

The drive was about 30 minutes. Ant took London to a beautiful park in Niagara Falls NY. As they walked along the pathway she noticed something very interesting. You have to be kidding me! Say it isn't so! Oh my God I have never! Like a kid in a candy store she was about to take her first Helicopter ride above the falls into NYC.

This is so dope! Tell me I'm dreaming.

No! Not at all. Just wait till we land.

It gets better?

It gets better!

The ride was roughly forty five minutes to an hour and Cupid was not happy. As soon as she was able to get down she pooped a big ole' pile of poop. Luckily wipes were supplied by the pilots assistant. Everything was set and as beautiful as it could be. They walked holding hands down a beautiful pathway to a gated section that read private. Once they approached the gate London could see a beach area with a tent and blankets laid out. The table was already set, with swimwear to follow. Are you hungry first or do you want to get wet some?

Hmmmm! LET'S GET WET!

While letting go of Ant's hand, and dropping Cupid's leash, London rushes over to put on the beautiful bathing suite Ant supplied. He picked Cupid up and shuffled over to join in on the activities.

Don't get my hair wet! You know I'm not one to be out in public looking like who shot the kid. Hahahaha.

Yes I know and so what if it gets wet!

What!

You heard me. You think I didn't prepare for that don't you. Well of course I would if I planned to bring you to the water. SPLASH!

Oh so you want to play huh? London splashed Ant right back!

So is my London having fun yet?

WHAT! I'M SUPER GEEKED!

Okay. Well how was lunch?

That salad was everything! Between the fruits and vegetables I was beginning to feel like you're trying to tell me I'm fat or something.

Hahahaha! Hell know your just right for me. I just did my research on what types of fruits and vegetables help fight cancers. I told you I love you and I was going to show you just how much. Welp we have to get out of here, as it's going to take an hour to get back home and we have a reservation at "Salvatore's" for 9 pm.

Um that's a little late for dinner you think?

Well maybe, but you'll see. Plus you have to get your hair re-done. We are expected to arrive at "Salvatore's" for the pre-show at 8, if that helps.

Pre-show? I've never heard of a pre-show before a dinner, like what's that?

Well there is a first for everything. I just hope that this will be the first of many more things to come.

Ring. Ring. Ring.

Hello?

Hi London. I just wanted to tell you thank you for being the only woman who cared about me. Oh and I'm sorry about your friend cousin. I really am. I'm going home in a couple of days and I wanted to know if you wouldn't mind coming to see me?

Well ah. Ummm. Sir I'm kind of busy right now. I'll call you and talk to you about that tomorrow sometime okay?

Oh so you just gone leave me now? I need you London. I'm sorry, I really am. Suddenly London's mood dampers and Ant picked right up on it. As happy as she was, she knew she actually loved both men. She didn't like seeing Sir need her, but she damn sure felt like a queen with Ant. Sir I'm sorry but I'm just going to have to talk with you tomorrow.

You okay babe?

Yes I'm fine.

We don't have to do anything else if you don't want to, you know that.

I'm fine. I wouldn't dare interrupt what you have managed to plan for nothing. I must say this is the best time I have ever had in my life, and I want to enjoy every minute of it. Suddenly a big smile popped back on her face and she leaned over initiating the kiss herself this time. Ant was finally feeling like he was getting somewhere and that maybe his last surprise would be everything he wanted and more.

Upon landing Ant, Cupid and London jump back in his car. While attempting to head back home he makes a quick detour. Shorty can I show you something real quick before we head to the house.

Why certainly.

About 20 minutes into the drive Ant pulls up to this beautiful home. Hey hand me cupid. She's our daughter for right now. Hahaha.

Oh is she?

Yes she is!

Well this home is beautiful. Who lives here?

Come on.

Oh you just going to go inside some random people's house I see. Shit! I bet I'm not going to jail with you. Huh, I'll wait in the car.

No silly come on. Buford we're here!

Buford. Okay what part of the game is this?

Hello Ms. London. Sir Anthony tells me so much about you.

Oh does he?

Yes, which is why he wanted to see what your thoughts were on this home before he buys it.

Home! Buy it! Aww shit now we know who really has the bread don't we.

Well let's start. Since you are on a specific time scale you can view each room on the monitor above. As you can see the home is equipped with the most current alarm & security system. It has Three and a half bathrooms, four bedrooms. Wait actually it is six, but the gentleman told me two would more than likely be office space. There is a well, organized area off of the front room, which can converted into either a playroom or a den. The back yard is already equipped with entertainment as the last owners enjoyed swimming, and acrobatics.

This house is amazing. I'm sure your mom, kids and brother will be happy with this choice.

As Ant knew that's where London would go, he thought mission accomplished. Buford we have to leave, but keep your phone on. If I call then you know it's a go. Should you not hear from me, you might need to send someone out to check on me.

Okay will do. Take care and have fun!

As I plan on it!

Both leave and head now to London's. Bae that house is amazing. I can't wait to come over and visit.

Oh you coming over to visit huh?

Yup I sure am.

Well what if I have a girlfriend. I mean you haven't told me you want anything to do with me, as I keep trying.

London frowns her face and then giggles as she realizes she just got jealous. Hmmm okay well she's just going to have to accept our bond. We'll always be the best of friends. Ant's expression on his face starts to change while London thinks to self, two can play this game.

Finally they arrive at the house. I need a quick nap!

Girl you should have went to sleep on that helicopter ride or better yet in the car. Come on we have to get ready. I know by now your craving meat because I sure as hell am.

Right! As soon as London opens the door she sees garment bags and boxes laid neatly on the dining room table, plus the house was spic and span clean. Hmmm so you managed to get my mom in on this too?

How'd you know?

Any child knows the way their mother cleans especially me!

Okay so let's get ready. Kia and Alisha will be returning, along with my barber Chris and my brother Mikey of course.

Oh okay so this is how you giving it up. Not to mention your even getting yourself pampered in my house with me. Hahahaha!

Well a man's got to do what a man's got to do.

Ding dong! Ding dong!

I'll get it. You just finish up your shower. Hey glad you all were on time. Okay she'll be out of the shower shortly and you ladies can join her upstairs. You guys know me. I'll be in and out in a quick five, ready to get trimmed. Everybody has their clothes?

Yup!

We do

Okay cool.

As everyone gets dressed, trimmed, pressed and curled, they all managed to look amazing.

Everyone looked amazing. London was so stunned by the gown she was wearing she didn't even pay attention to how everyone else was dressed, except Ant that is. As the limo pulls up to "Salvatore's" everyone goes in first except for London and Ant.

Well mom I hope this all goes according to our plan. I prayed and you provided me with the strength, idea, and income. Here goes! Shorty are you ready to go in?

Yes I am! London was feeling like a queen. While fighting back tears of joy she still was mesmerized by the way she and Ant looked together and all of his efforts to impress her.

I have to take this call. Just stand right here and wait to be escorted in and I'll be in shortly.

London says okay and follows the waiter into the private ballroom area.

This sure is nice just to have dinner with a few friends, but where are they, and where is Ant. The room was crowded as she began to look around. Suddenly she began to see other familiar faces. Hey uncle Raymond. I didn't know you were coming. When did you get here and you look very dapper if I must say.

Why thank you my favorite niece. You look astounding yourself. I'm here on a date with your auntie, dad and mom.

My dad and mom?

Yes ma'am!

Let me see.

Instantly a curtain open up and reveals as to why the room was divided. Everyone looked amazing. Mommy! London's daughter Sincere runs up to hug her. Are you happy mommy, because you look absolutely beautiful.

Why yes baby I am.

Okay well do me a big favor and keep this between me and you for now. Just say yes to Mr. Anthony okay? Sincere runs off giggling as the lights go dim and the room is instantly silenced.

May I have your attention please! Anthony is standing on the stage looking fine as hell, wearing a tuxedo all white with a pink, yellow and white carnation commanding attention from the audience. As you are all aware as to why this event was planned I wanted to take this opportunity and say it myself. Today we all come together to celebrate life. As it is not always filled with roses it can be. God gives us journeys so that one day we will find our kingdom. My brother and I grew up parentless and misfits. People's expectations of me were to be killed or imprisoned. Though I may have been a thug, street dealer and done things only I know of, I never turned my back on God. Night after night I prayed to be delivered. I prayed for my kingdom and by God almighty he provided it!

The room is filled with tears as everyone feels Anthony's heart felt speech.

The only thing missing was my queen. Anthony steps off stage and walks up to London who is standing dead center alone in the middle of the floor. When I saw I knew than you were for me. I tried to fight it but you kept appearing to me. Even when I thought walking away while you were in need, which I highly regret and wish never happened, you played in the back of my mind continuously. I knew I couldn't live without you. That very moment I saw you in that room with life, I knew why you were spared. You are my queen and I am your king. While getting down on one knee, Siyion walks over and hands Ant a box. London will you marry me?

By now it was obvious, and she knew where her heart really was. In less than twenty four hours, he managed to give her all that she had ever dreamed of. Instantly recalling what her daughter Sincere had asked. London said it and said loud and clear YESSSSSSSSS!

With a room full of emotion happiness had finally arrived. Buford walked up to the couple and says: I do believe these keys belong to you Mrs. Jackson.

Wait! You mean to tell me, you were planning to buy that house if I said yes?

Well?

YESSSSSSSSSSSS! YESSSSSSSS! YESSSSSSSSSS!

London couldn't stop crying tears of joy. Everyone was present even Nasir's mom and sister Jazz. Congratulations girl. You deserve that!

This story was designed to tell you that fairy tales do come true! If the relationship is Cancerous than he/she is not for you. No woman or man should be made to feel less then. No woman or man should fear being who God made them, or settle for not what he has for you. It is okay to start over! It is okay to walk away! It is even more okay to love thy self and just wait on who God has. I hope you enjoyed and if anything are empowered!

"Abuse is the devil. Don't fall victim to its charm"

By Yours Truly

Tkay TheAuthor

Please be on the look-out for more great and amazing reads.

My next release will be "Bravery is Beauty"

This story will be a e-book read only, based on my real life struggle and fight with Breast Cancer. Minority women are the largest population effected by this deceitful disease, as we are also the least educated on our rights, wishes, and plans to beat this beast. I plan on becoming a vessel to help women in need, who are currently battling with this monster, beat this monster and/or have loss someone dear too it!

It's time we took a look in the mirror and obtained the resources needed to live happily ever after. Family wise, health wise, spiritually and more. I am available via www.Tkaytheauthor.org for public speaking, group counsels or individual/personal discussion's. Please make sure to leave reliable contact information and allow 48 hours to receive follow up contact!

Should you enjoy other great and amazing reads, here's two from my home town "Buffalo NY".

Ms. Laura Jackson Best Seller of "Destination Queendom"

Author Cassie Solomon "Wrong Lover" & so many more!

The End!

Dream big! Make it happen & go for it!

Made in the USA
Middletown, DE
06 July 2021